"How do I tell these people we can't help them?"

Brady reached forward and touched Josie's arm again, letting his hand rest there for a moment. In the old days, he'd have hugged her close and given her the reassurance she was asking for. But this would have to do. "I don't think they think that at all. Everyone in town has been commenting about how pleased they are that you're stepping up to save the stables. It means a lot to everyone, and I'm sure, if your father were here, it would have meant a lot to him."

"Maybe." She kicked at the ground. "Funny how quickly I revert to being that scared little girl."

He gave her arm a final squeeze. "I know it's not the same, but I'm here for you." The warm smile he got in return gave him hope.

"Thank you. Things may have changed between us, but it does feel good to know I'm not alone."

Danica Favorite loves the adventure of living a creative life. She loves to explore the depths of human nature and follow people on the journey to happily-ever-after. Though the journey is often bumpy, those bumps refine imperfect characters as they live the lives God created them for. Oops, that just spoiled the endings of Danica's stories. Then again, getting there is all the fun. Find her at danicafavorite.com.

Books by Danica Favorite

Love Inspired

Shepherd's Creek

Journey to Forgiveness

Double R Legacy

The Cowboy's Sacrifice
His True Purpose
A True Cowboy
Her Hidden Legacy

Three Sisters Ranch

Her Cowboy Inheritance
The Cowboy's Faith
His Christmas Redemption

Visit the Author Profile page at LoveInspired.com for more titles.

Journey to Forgiveness

Danica Favorite

LOVE INSPIRED
INSPIRATIONAL ROMANCE

LOVE INSPIRED®
INSPIRATIONAL ROMANCE

Recycling programs
for this product may
not exist in your area.

ISBN-13: 978-1-335-58605-6

Journey to Forgiveness

Copyright © 2022 by Danica Favorite

For questions and comments about the quality of this book, please contact us
at CustomerService@Harlequin.com.

Love Inspired
22 Adelaide St. West, 41st Floor
Toronto, Ontario M5H 4E3, Canada
www.LoveInspired.com

Printed in U.S.A.

Then came Peter to him, and said, Lord,
how oft shall my brother sin against me,
and I forgive him? till seven times? Jesus saith
unto him, I say not unto thee, Until seven times:
but, Until seventy times seven.

—*Matthew* 18:21–22

For the real Kayla. Though you can be exasperating, you are also a constant source of inspiration to me with your bravery, your wit, your tender heart and your passion. I love you.

Chapter One

Josie Shepherd pulled up in front of the main barn at the Shepherd's Creek Equestrian Complex. The only reason she'd relented on her promise to never return to Hidden Valley, the small town nestled in the Colorado mountains where she'd grown up, was because her cousin Abigail had begged her. Even then, she'd skipped the memorial service and was only here for the will reading she'd been told she had to attend.

She got out of the car and adjusted her skirt. For a moment, she regretted her decision to wear a dress and heels, but what was done was done. Another outfit might have been more practical, but she wanted no trace of the old Josie here. It was bad enough having to face the memories. She was a new woman now, and she lived life her way, wore the clothes she wanted to wear and wasn't going to let this place change that, even for a moment.

She'd no sooner started for the barn when a familiar voice greeted her.

"Junior. I mean, Josie."

Her appearance hadn't been the only thing Josie had changed upon leaving. Her father had always wanted a son, and when it was clear a daughter was all he was going to get, he'd named her after himself. She'd grown up as Junior, and it wasn't until she left this place that she'd been able to carve out her own identity.

Abigail. Josie smiled at her cousin, grateful to begin the visit with a friendly face. Most of the people here, she didn't want to see or talk to.

Abigail strode toward her and gave her a big hug. It felt awkward at first, but then Josie leaned into the embrace. Abigail was the only one Josie still talked to, and not very often. Abigail had been like a big sister/surrogate mother to her growing up, since Josie's own mom had passed away in childbirth, and none of Josie's problems with her father were Abigail's fault.

When Abigail released her, she said, "We missed you at the memorial service."

"I told you I wasn't going to come."

The disappointed expression on Abigail's face was the exact same one she'd often given Josie during her teenage years. "I know, but I'd hoped you would've changed your mind."

Even though they'd already had this conversation on the phone, Abigail's gentle rebuke stung. Abigail, of all people, should have understood how difficult this was for her. When Josie left, her father told her she was dead to him. He had been the one to send back everything to her unopened.

Now that he was dead, was she just supposed to forget all that?

Josie shook her head. "Coming here is hard enough for me. Let's get the papers signed and over with."

Abigail looked at her like she wanted to say something else but then stopped and stared in the other direction. Josie turned to see what Abigail had been looking at.

Brady King. The other reason she'd left. Brady had always told her he'd stand beside her to help her stand up to her father. That had been a lie.

She hated that he still looked good. Hated

that her heart still skipped a beat, even though she had a million reasons why it was completely inappropriate.

And one of them, the biggest one, was right beside him.

The teenage girl walking next to him.

All those years ago, when Maddie Antere claimed to be carrying Brady's baby, Josie had wanted to believe it was a lie, just like all the other things Maddie used to lie about. But apparently, Maddie had been telling the truth. Brady had confirmed it long ago, but it wasn't until now, seeing the man she'd once thought she was going to marry, and his daughter, that it really hit her. Her throat tightened, and as much as she'd told herself throughout the years that she was completely over Brady, she hadn't expected to feel so much pain at seeing him again.

The pain intensified as Maddie, the teen's mother, walked up to Brady and put her arm around him. Though Abigail had told Josie that Brady never married Maddie, they clearly still had a close relationship. It surprised Josie to once again feel a pang of jealousy when she saw them together.

"You should have told me they were going

to be here," Josie told Abigail under her breath.

"I was afraid you wouldn't come if I did."

Her unapologetic tone reminded Josie of how bad the whole betrayal had been.

Her father might have told others that Josie was his world, but if that had been true, why had he been okay with Brady's infidelity? Worse, her father had given Brady a job so he would have a way to support Maddie and their baby.

No, that wasn't the worst. Brady had known how bad her relationship with her father was, so on top of being unfaithful to her with her worst enemy, he'd gone to work for the very man they'd planned on leaving behind when starting their new lives.

Brady had chosen the people who'd hurt her the most.

Josie took a deep breath. It didn't matter now. That was in the past. Her father had wanted a dramatic will reading, so here she was.

She'd be facing almost every person who'd ever hurt her, except her father. And Abigail, the only reason she'd been willing to come.

Fighting the desire to get back in her car and drive away, she walked into the barn, to the small conference room in the office area, taking in the familiar faces. They were all staring at her, as she knew they would, considering she hadn't been back for fifteen years. Though everyone looked a bit older, it seemed none of them had changed—just her, she supposed.

"Junior." Hal Evans, who had been her father's best friend, greeted her warmly, as if her absence had been a mere vacation.

"What are you going to do with the stables?" he asked. "It'll be so good, having you back. Your father always wanted you to run this place."

"I'm not staying," she said. "I only came as a courtesy to Abigail, who said she needed me here. But I'll be headed back home when this is over."

Hal looked at her funny. "But this is your home. Who will run the stables if you don't?"

Josie shook her head. "I don't know, and I don't care. It's not my problem."

"You would say that," Maddie said, entering the room. "That's always been what's wrong with you. You've never cared about anyone but yourself."

Of course that would be Maddie's response. Josie had spent her entire childhood being tormented by Maddie. Maddie had always strived to undermine Josie, making her life miserable and doing everything she could to one-up her.

But surely, after fifteen years, Maddie had been able to let it go. After all, Maddie had won.

"What does it matter to you?" Josie asked. "You should be happy I'm not staying. You've gotten everything you wanted in life, so why can't you forget whatever childish feud we had?"

The flash in Maddie's eyes told Josie that the other woman was spoiling for a fight. Brady put his hand on Maddie's arm. "Let it go."

Brady turned his attention back to Josie. "I'm so sorry for your loss," he said. "I know you two had your differences, but it's a loss nonetheless."

Josie shrugged, trying not to let Brady's comment about them having their differences sting so much. If only her issues with her father were as simple as "having their differences." No, her problems with her father were far deeper than that. He'd never complimented her when she excelled and he'd berated her when she erred. He'd pushed her into a life she didn't plan on pursuing and turned a deaf ear when she talked about the future she really cared about. She'd wanted to get out of the stables and this town as soon as she could. The old Brady knew better. How had she loved this man so much when he'd clearly not loved her at all?

"My father hasn't been part of my life for fifteen years," Josie said. "I'm sorry, but I don't feel the same level of grief as the rest of you. It's probably not appropriate that I be here, except Abigail insisted."

The edges of Brady's eyes softened, and he nodded slowly. "We were all hoping that the two of you would resolve your problems. I'm sure it must be difficult to have lost him without any closure."

Josie fought the urge to roll her eyes. First of all, Brady had no right trying to comfort her. They weren't boyfriend/girlfriend anymore, and they certainly weren't even friends. Secondly, none of these people could pretend to understand her emotions about her father's death. She didn't need closure. She had received plenty of therapy for that. All Josie needed was to get whatever show this was over with and get back to her life.

Still, as she looked around the room at all the red-rimmed eyes, she couldn't bring herself to say something that would offend any of them.

"I think we're all dealing with it as best as we can," she said, giving Brady a small smile.

He came at her like he was going to try to hug her, and she quickly stepped away. What right did he have to think that she'd welcome a hug from him?

And yet, part of her craved it. Until he'd betrayed her, the safest place had always been in his arms. Why, after all this time, could he still have an impact on her?

He gestured at an empty chair. "You should take a seat. It looks like we were the last people to arrive, and I'm sure everyone is eager to get started."

Even though it was the fake politeness of a man who no longer knew her, it still hurt for him to act like nothing had happened between them. If their time together had meant anything to him, he'd know just how hard this was for her.

The worst part was, she shouldn't have cared so much about Brady and his reactions. How could she feel any sense of attachment to the man who'd betrayed her with her worst enemy?

As soon as Josie found a seat, Albert Maitland, who had been the family attorney and a close friend of her father's since before Josie had been born, cleared his throat. As he read through the will, Josie tried not to roll her eyes at the way her father had nickel-and-dimed everything. Though he'd given Abigail the house—with an odd provision that she only owned the dwelling itself—the other gifts were small potatoes. A hundred dollars here, a hundred dollars there—it hardly seemed worth the time and expense of going through probate to give everyone their share. Everyone else in the room seemed gratified that he'd remembered them enough to provide them with even such a small bequest.

If anything, this proved just how much Josie didn't belong here. All these people thought her father was a wonderful hero of a man, and all Josie could remember was how badly he treated her.

"'The remainder of my estate,'" Albert said, "'including the stables, all of our property, all of my other assets, all the animals, all of the items contained within the barns and house and all other outbuildings, as well as any remaining cash in my account, I leave to my daughter, Joseph Stephen Shepherd Junior.'"

Josie felt sick. With all the insulting bequests, she'd been expecting a slap in the face where he'd say what a horrible daughter she'd been and how she deserved absolutely nothing and wasn't worthy of the name. But this—this was almost worse. He'd given her everything. She looked over at Abigail, who was silently crying. The tears running down her cousin's face made Josie's heart hurt. Her father had given Abigail the house, but Josie had been given the power over it. Abigail hadn't even been given the contents of the house, just the building and not the land upon which it sat.

And in a flash of insight, Josie knew. She understood. This was her father's way of forcing her to come back. Big Joe had known that Josie would not throw her cousin out on the street. She wasn't going to take anything from any of these people, who had worked so hard.

"What if I don't accept?" Josie said. "These people all deserve it far more than I do, and it's not fair that he left me everything. I want them all to have it. How do you distribute it between the rest of them?"

Surely, this would take away some of the angry stares directed at her.

Albert scratched his head but didn't look surprised by her question. "Then everything will be sold and donated to charity. Big Joe's wish was for you to take responsibility for the stables."

Josie couldn't bear to look at her cousin.

Abigail had devoted her life to the stables, and it was incredibly unfair that Josie benefited over her.

"What if I sell it?" Josie asked. "Is there anything in the will preventing me from selling?"

Albert looked surprised, and the gasps from the rest of the people gathered made her realize that no one had expected her to say that.

But why would they? None of them knew her anymore. They hadn't really known her to begin with. That was the trouble. Proof she had to leave.

Scratching his head again, Albert said, "Well, I guess you could do so. He never said anything about that."

He looked around the room, then his gaze settled back on Josie. "But if you sell, what about all these people and their jobs? What about the people who board their horses here? What about the kids who develop their riding skills and confidence through all the competitions the stables enter? If you sell this place, that will all end."

He was using the wrong argument to keep her from selling. All those reasons were exactly why she wanted to sell.

"No offense, but I don't believe in the stables' mission of developing the youth. I think they do a terrible job of it, doing more harm than good. I'm the director of a rec center in the Denver metro area, and I've studied child psychology. So I know what it means to develop the lives of young people, and I'm already doing that. I don't need the stables to accomplish that goal."

"What about people's jobs?" Maddie screeched. "You might have your big-city job to go back to, but what about the rest of us? You are so selfish. Thinking about yourself, and not what anybody here needs."

She was selfish? Maddie was the one freaking out over whether or not she would have an income. It wasn't like Hidden Valley was all that far from civilization, anyway. Sure, it was a bit of a commute, but it wasn't like when Josie was growing up here, when it was truly the middle of nowhere. The cities around them had grown, developed, and were spreading out toward the tiny community of Hidden Valley. They could all find jobs.

"I didn't realize you worked for the stables," Josie said.

"I don't," Maddie said. "While I have a good job at the nursing home, there's Brady to think about. If he doesn't have work, he can't pay his child support. Do you think I can support Kayla on my own? No. I can't. But you don't care about my child. I'm sure you don't care about the children of anybody else here. We have families, and you will throw it all away because of some stupid vendetta you have against your father."

Brady put his hand on Maddie's arm, but Maddie pulled away. "No. I'm not going to shut up and be nice. I'm sorry if the rest of you want to act like this is wonderful, the prodigal coming home, but we all know that the fight between Big Joe and Junior started with Junior throwing a hissy fit at the Sundown Horse Show."

The room fell silent again, and the sick feeling in Josie's stomach only grew worse.

Was that what everyone thought? That this was all because of some hissy fit at a competition?

It was true that her final public fight with her father had been at a horse show. But her differences with him were much bigger than that.

Josie hadn't realized that others had interpreted it as a petty disagreement. But now was not the time to defend herself.

Brushing a stray tear from her eye, Josie

looked at Maddie. "If that's what you believe, then you don't know the first thing about my father or me. But the truth is, you never did know me. You've always had this picture in your mind of who you think I was, but it wasn't true. The situation is way more complicated than anyone here knows, and I'm doing my best to be respectful of everyone else's feelings, so the least you can do is respect mine."

"If you respected people's feelings, you wouldn't want to sell the stables," Maddie snapped, prompting murmurs of agreement from everyone else gathered in the room.

She realized that there was not one friendly or sympathetic face as she looked around. Even Abigail appeared disgusted with her, and her cousin had been the only person to support her when Josie had left.

Even worse, she hated seeing the disappointment on Brady's face. Why did she care what he thought? She had nothing to prove to him.

"You can't sell," Albert said. "The only people willing to buy something this big would be a developer. They'd put condos and tract homes on this place. We keep fighting to save this area from becoming overdeveloped, and you'll be handing it right to them. Please don't do this to us."

Though she was sympathetic to the idea of not wanting to develop the area, it wasn't her call what happened to the land. If her father hadn't wanted the stables to fall into the hands of a developer, he would've done something to stop it.

That was the thing. They were all blaming her, but her father was the one who had done it.

"I can't run the stables," Josie said softly. "I have my own life. I work with my own youth organization. You talk about all the people here who need me, but you don't understand that I already have people I'm helping. What about them? We have over five thousand children enrolled in our programs. Are you asking me to abandon them?"

Her words didn't seem to elicit sympathy from any of them, and at this point, everyone was probably too emotionally overwrought to think or discuss things rationally. Even Josie was not in the right place to make a rational decision at this point.

"I'm sorry," she said. "I know this was my father's last-ditch effort to get me home, but it failed."

She turned to Albert. "Is there anything else I need to hear right now? I need time to think. I'll call you in the morning, and we can set up a time to sort all this out."

Albert nodded slowly, so she turned and walked out of the room. If stares were daggers, she had a million of them in her back right now. But what was she supposed to do? Giving them what they wanted would ruin the life she'd built for herself. Maintaining her life seemed like it was going to ruin theirs. Was there any way they could find a compromise?

She was halfway to the car when she heard Brady calling her.

"Junior. I mean, Josie. Can we talk?"

Brady hadn't expected to be hit with so many feelings at seeing Josie again. It had never felt right calling her "Junior," and when they were younger, Josie used to play around with nicknames other than the one she had. But her father made it very clear to everyone that she was, and always would be, Junior. Josie fit her. It was feminine, soft and pretty, just like her.

Seeing her in front of him now, dressed exactly like she'd stepped out of one of those magazines she used to read as a teenager, he could see that Josie Shepherd was exactly the woman she used to tell him she wanted to be.

Beautiful, feminine, someone who had charted her own life.

Funny how quickly the old feelings he thought he'd banished had returned. But that wasn't what was important now.

"Josie!" he called out to her again, as she appeared to have not heard him the first time. Or was ignoring him. He had to talk to her.

Josie couldn't sell the stables.

She hadn't been around to see the changes, so to her, it was a lot of bad memories. However, everyone in that room knew what a valuable program this was for the kids. He just had to convince her of it.

Josie had been savaged in there, and while Brady should have done more to stand up for her, he'd been in too much shock over the situation to say or do anything.

Part of him didn't blame Josie for her reaction.

Brady had known how difficult things were for her growing up. He understood her motivation. He just knew the lives that would be ruined if she sold the stables.

He had to convince her that the stables were worth keeping.

Brady caught up with her when she was almost to her car. One of those environmentally friendly things that was as useless on a ranch as a miniskirt was on a horse.

"Josie!" he yelled again, and this time she turned. Her eyes were red, like she was about to cry and was just waiting to get to the car to let her tears loose. He knew that expression. Had seen it probably hundreds of times at riding competitions.

"Please talk to me," he said.

Brady had once been Josie's confidant, and what he'd seen had been enough for him to understand that the relationship with her father was far more complicated than what most knew.

Few people ever saw that side of Joe's relationship with Josie, so it was no wonder they were so perplexed at her lack of emotion over her father's passing.

Which left it to Brady to convince her that saving the stables was about more than her relationship with her father. And, as much as he hated to admit it, was more important than the pain he'd caused her.

Fine. He'd admit it. Brady had broken Josie's heart. One stupid drunken mistake, and he'd lost the love of his life.

The lift to her chin as she looked at him now reminded him of when she'd asked him if it was true about Maddie's pregnancy. She hadn't let him speak beyond his "yes," and she was going to avoid talking to him now if she could.

"I need space," Josie said. "We can talk another time."

Brady knew her well enough that if she had anything to say about it, another time would be never.

The crunch of gravel behind him made Brady turn.

"Please don't go. I need you home," Abigail said.

When Brady returned his gaze to Josie, tears had begun falling down her face. He took a step forward to offer her comfort, but she moved back and her fancy high heel twisted, causing her to fall.

"Are you okay?" Brady rushed to help her up. Abigail wasn't far behind.

"I can do it myself," Josie said, struggling to get back on her feet.

The same stubborn woman. The same grit and determination written all over her face that had been one of the reasons he'd fallen in love with her in the first place. Fifteen years apart wasn't enough to make him forget just how much she'd meant to him.

Getting her to agree to keep the stables running seemed like an impossible dream, given that she wouldn't even let him help her up.

She'd be insulted if he said so, but the apple didn't fall far from the tree.

It was quickly obvious, though, that by the way she was struggling, Josie's left ankle had been seriously injured.

"You need to see a doctor," Brady said.

"I'm fine."

So much vulnerability under her strong words. He'd been one of the few she'd ever let see that side of her, and even now, he immediately recognized it for what it was.

Josie needed help, but she wasn't going to reveal her weakness by admitting it.

She used to let him help her, but he'd stupidly gone and ruined that.

Abigail had already whipped out her cell phone.

"I told you I'm fine," Josie said, her voice almost a screech. Tears started rolling down her face freely, and it was probably a combination of both physical and emotional pain.

Brady took a step back. "Then walk over to me."

An unfair challenge, but by the way she favored her right side, Brady was almost certain her left ankle was broken, if not severely sprained. As part of his duties at the stables, he'd taken several first-aid courses, leading to him becoming a paramedic for the local volunteer fire department. He'd handled enough ankle injuries to know that Josie was hurt far more seriously than she was letting on.

But the only way he could convince her of that would be if she failed this test.

Sure enough, Josie could only take one step before she winced with what was probably excruciating pain.

When he walked over to her, Josie didn't resist. Abigail had stepped away and was talking on the phone, probably to Bob Francis, the local doctor who helped with medical needs at the stables from time to time.

Brady put his arm around Josie. "I'm going to help you over to the bench, where I can do a better job of examining your ankle."

The set of Josie's jaw as she nodded told him that she was in too much pain to argue.

It didn't take more than a cursory examination to know Josie had a serious injury. Brady waved Abigail over.

"I'm pretty sure it's broken," he said. "Tell Doc we'll meet him at the clinic. I'm going to help her into my truck. While we're doing that, grab an ice pack so we can keep the swelling down."

Josie looked up at him, a forlorn expression filling her face. "Maybe it's just a bad sprain," she said.

"Even if it's just a sprain, you're going to have to stay off of it for a while. Do you have someone at home who will be able to help you for a few weeks?"

The question was supposed to be of medical concern, but he had more than a professional reason for asking, if he was honest with himself.

While he was being honest, the slow shake of her head made him feel better, even though he should be more concerned about her being alone with an injury.

"I know there's a lot of past between us," Brady said. "But you've got to let me help you here."

Mercifully, she didn't argue as he put his arm around her and assisted her into his truck. From the way her brow creased, he could tell she was in a lot of pain. He couldn't give her anything for it until they talked to the doctor, but maybe he could distract her.

"What have you been doing with your life since you left?" Brady asked.

He tried telling himself that he was just being polite, but the truth was, he wanted to know everything.

"We're not friends anymore," Josie said stiffly.

Even though Josie was right, her words stung on a deeper level than he'd imagined they would, considering the two of them hadn't spoken in fifteen years.

"Maybe not," he admitted. "But we can at least be polite. I'd like to hear about your life now."

He wanted to add that maybe they could find a way to save the stables so it wouldn't impact her life, but the hard set to her jaw told him that this was the wrong time.

"I told you," Josie said. "We're not friends anymore. My life is none of your business."

As the tears rolled down her cheeks, he wished he could take her in his arms and tell her it was going to be okay, that they'd figure out a way to fix things together.

But Josie was right. They weren't friends anymore.

Chapter Two

Broken. And if Josie stayed off it and kept it immobilized, she wouldn't require surgery. So much for her vanity in wanting to show everyone how different she was now. The expensive heels she just had to have had become her downfall.

Which was why she was here the next day, nestled in her old bedroom, which had been left completely unchanged since the day she left.

Abigail entered the room, carrying a tray with tea, some mini sandwiches that were probably left over from the funeral and an assortment of cookies, as well as some veggies and dip.

Thoughtful, as always.

"I'm sorry if I was rude yesterday," Josie

said. "It's been a lot to take in, and I wasn't expecting any of this."

For a moment, Abigail stood there, like she was choosing her words. Then she said, "He's always made it clear that he favored you. We would have done anything for his affection, but it was always about you. He gave you everything, and you want to destroy it."

Her cousin's voice shook as she spoke, and it tore at Josie's insides. Abigail was the one person who should have been able to understand. She'd seen all the fights and how hard Joe had been on Josie.

"I didn't ask for him to give me the stables," Josie said. "I have a whole life that I can't pick up and leave, even if I wanted to. He should have left everything to you and Laura."

Her answer only made Abigail's expression of distress even worse. "He wasn't speaking to Laura because he didn't like the man she married."

The anger in Abigail's voice made Josie feel sick. Typical of her father. Stop talking to someone when he didn't like what they were doing. Just like he'd done with her.

"I'm sorry," Josie said. "I didn't know. The last I heard, he was giving her away, and Brady was the best man. I couldn't face them."

Josie had agonized over her decision. But having to deal with her father and Brady was too much. Though she'd given up any hope of a future with him the day he acknowledged Maddie's baby was his, it didn't mean that seeing him still didn't hurt. Even now, the ache in her heart was almost too much to bear.

How could she still have these feelings after fifteen years, when she had been the wounded party?

"You refused to go to her wedding," Abigail said. "Your grudges were more important than your love for your cousin. And now, because of that same grudge, you're willing to destroy people's lives."

Because they'd all learned her father's silent treatment approach, Laura had stopped speaking to Josie when Josie had refused to come to the wedding. But Josie hadn't been emotionally able to handle her father or Brady. Laura's husband, Cash, was Brady's best friend. She'd tried to explain to Laura, but Laura had called her selfish. That seemed to be everyone's default opinion when Josie tried to set boundaries between her and her father.

"I know I seem coldhearted," Josie said. "I don't want to destroy the stables. That's never been my wish. But please understand—I've been through a lot. And I would think that you've seen enough of it that you would understand, too."

The expression on Abigail's face softened slightly. "I know. I'm sorry. It's just a blow to think of losing the stables."

"The stables don't represent the same thing to me. It's taken years of therapy to get past a lot of it."

Obviously, she still wasn't past it. She'd thought she was, but she clearly still had a lot more work to do. When she got back home, she would set up another appointment with her therapist.

"We all did the best we could," Abigail said, sounding like she felt Josie was to blame.

"It wasn't your responsibility," Josie said. "He was supposed to be the parent. I am extremely grateful for everything you've done, but this is on him, not you. I promise you, I'll find a way to fix the situation. You won't be without a home or income."

Abigail shook her head slowly. "It's not

about that. God will provide, just as He always has. The thing that I'm most concerned about is what's going to happen to the stables. To the community it serves. Don't you care?"

"We've been through this. I'm already helping youth. I don't have the capacity to take on anything else."

"Then why would you take it from this community? Yes, your community has what it needs. But Hidden Valley? You'd be taking the only good thing it has."

"Whether or not it's good is up for debate," Josie said. "Others might have had a good experience with it, but can you see where I might feel differently? And it's not just my personal feelings. I have a college degree to back it up."

The sadness on Abigail's face made it clear she shouldn't have mentioned her degree. Josie hadn't been the only one who wanted to go to college. She'd just been the only one to defy her father to actually do it.

"I'm sorry," Josie said. "I didn't mean to touch on a sore subject."

Abigail's eyes filled with tears. "I may just have a high-school education, but I know that our community is better for having the stables. And maybe if you took a look at it, not as someone who has a grudge from the past, but as someone who cares about keeping a community alive, you might see things differently."

Josie took a deep breath. "I would never intentionally hurt you. You're right on an important point, though. Just because I had a bad experience doesn't mean that all this is a complete waste. That said, Abigail, even if I agree the stables' program is valuable, I can't drop everything in my life to come back here to run it."

Though she'd focused on how terrible her father had been, the saving grace in the program had always been Abigail, her encouragement and gentle approach. Back in the day, Josie would have said Brady would be able to do a lot for the stables as well. But that was before his betrayal. Had she even known him? What kind of man was he now? She wasn't sure her heart was willing to find out.

"At least try," Abigail said. "Maybe we can work something out. Your father wasn't in the best of health the past few years, anyway. He left most of the operations to Brady. There were many things that your father and Brady disagreed on, and maybe if Brady could run the whole thing himself, things could go on as they were, or even better. You said it yourself. You don't want anything. You don't want his money. So if you leave things as they were, except for your father not being here, we could go on, just as we were before."

It wasn't a half-bad idea. She'd be fulfilling the terms of her father's will by taking ownership of and keeping the stables running. Nothing would change other than giving Brady full responsibility. Knowing her father and Brady, they had probably butted heads over a lot of things, which probably hurt the stables.

Could it be as simple as letting things continue as they had been?

But that would also mean working with Brady.

Even if she was merely the owner in name only, she still had to do her due diligence and make sure everything was done properly. The last thing she needed was to be liable for anything going wrong at the stables. She could be an absentee owner, just checking in from time to time.

"I'm not going to promise you anything, but I will consider it." She gestured at the crutches leaning against the wall. "Let's see how I can get around this place. Give me a tour and tell me about the changes. I'll get in touch with Brady and see what things look like from his perspective."

More tears filled Abigail's eyes. "Thank you. I know this means nothing to you, but if we could find a way to keep everything going, it would mean the world to me."

Josie scooted to the edge of the bed, swinging her legs over. Abigail handed her the crutches. The hardest of all the things she had to face here would be talking to Brady. If she agreed to Abigail's plan, she'd have to work closely with Brady. During the few months she'd stayed in town after Maddie's pregnancy was announced, she'd found all sorts of creative ways to avoid him. There'd be no avoiding him now. The only reason she was even considering this was Abigail.

As Brady supervised a lesson, he saw a familiar figure heading his way. Brady hadn't expected to see Josie walking around the property so soon. He thought she'd spend a couple of days sitting around and keeping her foot elevated, per the doctor's orders. But as eager as she had been to wash her hands of the place, he supposed the sooner she got this handled, the sooner she could go put up her foot in the comfortable home of hers, where she didn't have to worry about anyone else.

Maybe as she looked around, he could get her to fall back in love with the place and decide not to sell. Or God would touch her heart and make her realize that the stables weren't that bad after all.

Probably too much to hope that she'd see a way to forgive him. She'd barely looked at him or spoken to him on the trip to and from the clinic, and she'd insisted on seeing the doctor alone.

Alone.

That seemed to be the way of Josie's life now, from the best he could put together. The opposite of the time they'd grown up together, when friends and family had surrounded her. He might not have gotten to live the dream life he and Josie had planned, but the one he did have was full of people he cared about and who cared about him. Josie could have that again if she was willing to open her heart.

But could she get past the pain her father had caused, the pain he'd caused, to see that?

He glanced at his watch and saw that the lesson he was teaching was almost over. He gave the kids their final instructions, and once they were on their way back with the wranglers to put away the horses, Brady turned to see that Josie was still waiting in the stands.

He walked over to her, hating the butterflies in his stomach. Yes, it was partially nerves over what the future would hold. He'd talked to Abigail briefly the night before, and her gentle faith that the Lord would provide had reassured him at the time. But seeing Josie now, he knew the Lord's provision would have to be great. Worse, though, the butterflies were also about that girl he once held in his arms, the one he'd promised the world to and, in one rash decision, had completely let down.

It would be so much easier if he didn't feel anything for her anymore. He'd been the one to break her heart, not the other way around, and no matter how hard he tried, he hadn't been able to forget her. It would be so much easier if he felt nothing for her or even had the same hatred for her that she had for him. He couldn't call it love. After all, it had been fifteen years, and they were different people now. But there was definitely a fondness for the things they had once shared and deep regret on his part for the promises he'd broken.

Part of him wondered if her reasoning for wanting to get rid of this place was also about the pain he had caused her.

"I'm surprised to see you up and about," Brady said as he approached Josie and Abigail.

Josie shrugged. "I've never been one to sit around and do nothing. My coworkers all tease me because I've never seen any of the shows they talk about. Just feels lazy, spending hours in front of the television."

Brady laughed. She shared that trait with her father, who had refused to let the family own a TV for many years. He used to say that if they had time to waste staring at a box, they had time for extra training or chores. When they were teenagers, Josie used to sneak over to his house to watch TV with him and his family. A few years after Josie left, Brady had gotten a small television for Abigail to keep in her room, but it was still the only TV in the Shepherd house as far as Brady knew.

"So what do you do when you're not working?" he asked.

Josie shrugged. "A lot of things. I exercise, go on hikes and I'm part of a couple of different recreational sports leagues. I keep busy."

"Anything with horses?" he asked.

Josie shook her head. "Not since college. It's expensive to own a horse, and plus, my heart wasn't in it. There are a lot more activities that I find satisfaction in."

It was a shame she'd given up her horses. Josie had always loved the animals, much more than anything else he could remember. When they were ten, Josie had declared that she loved her horse so much that she was going to marry him. And when Brady informed her that people couldn't marry horses, Josie had said that she loved hers the best of all, and if she couldn't marry him, she wouldn't marry anyone.

Well, he supposed she'd remained true to the not-marrying-anyone part.

Funny how as much as she'd said she'd loved Blade at the time, she'd been able to walk away from him without a second thought. Blade had known when she'd gone. Because he was just a horse, he hadn't understood why Josie would leave him. He was never the same after that, and when the horse died a few years later, Brady would have sworn it was from a broken heart.

"What are you doing out here?" he asked.

Josie shrugged. "Figured I'd get a look at things, see what the operations were like now, how things have changed."

"She might let us keep things as they are, letting us run the place," Abigail said, her face bright with excitement.

"Is that so?" he asked. Unlike Abigail, he tried to keep his voice level because he didn't want to get his hopes up. But if there was a chance they could keep this place going, that would be the best of all without any major changes.

Josie turned to Abigail. "I told you I would consider it. Nothing's been decided yet." Then she returned her attention to Brady. "I'll be honest. I meant it when I said I didn't want to have anything to do with the stables. I'm not going to be selfish like my father and ruin a bunch of people's lives because I can't let go of the past. Still, I have a life of my own, and I'm not giving it up to save this place. So you're going to have to convince me that all of this will run fine on its own with little to no involvement on my part."

He stared at her for a moment, trying to process her words. Was she really saying she would hand over everything for him to manage? Ideally, that would be perfect. He had so many ideas of what he'd like to do with the stables, but Big Joe had always refused to consider anything that he hadn't thought of himself.

"That would be a dream come true," Brady said. "Everyone would get what they want.

We'd love for you to come home, but I understand why you wouldn't. Thank you for giving us the chance to remain."

Josie held up a hand. "I haven't made any decisions yet. As I said, you will have to prove to me that you can run this place without my involvement. I know how often my father was on the phone, dealing with this and that to run the stables. I don't have time for that."

Did Abigail hear the pain in Josie's voice the way he did? Did she remember all the times when Josie would say "Look at me, Dad," only for his back to be to her while he was talking to some business associate?

Brady wanted to make Josie fall in love with the place again. To see this as her home. But getting to keep the stables was the next best thing. He'd lived long enough without having her in his life. He'd figured out how to do that. He would find a way to prove to her that he could make the stables work.

If only letting go of Josie again didn't put a strange ache in his heart.

He held out his arm to her. "Let me start by taking you on a tour."

Josie reached for her crutches, and he grinned. She was still the same tough girl. As he walked her through the property to show her what had changed with the facilities since she'd been gone, he was impressed with how well she kept up.

"You handle the crutches like a pro," he said.

"I blew my knee out playing volleyball a couple of years ago," she said. "I had to have surgery, but I was on crutches for a couple of months. I guess, like riding a bike, you never forget."

At least the hostility in her tone had lessened from when he'd spoken to her the day before. Maybe she was giving this a real chance.

"Or like riding a horse," he said, opening the door to the stable where the horses were kept. He had hoped that she would comment on the horses, but she didn't say anything about them as she stepped through the doors.

"I see he's added on here," she said.

"Yes. He's always had room for the competition horses, but many of the people who board with us also wanted the option of having indoor stalls and were willing to pay for it. We were considering expanding before your father died because there's a waiting list for people who want indoor stall care."

He started telling her about the boarding

program, but realized she wasn't paying attention. Instead, she was staring at the stall where her old horse, Blade, had been kept.

"He died a couple of years after you left," Brady said. "The vet said it was colic, but I'm pretty sure it was a broken heart. He was never the same once you were gone."

Josie spun to face him. "Guilt-tripping me isn't going to convince me not to sell this place." She walked over to the stall and ran her fingers over the nameplate.

So much for easing tensions between them. He shouldn't have said that about Blade's passing, but the old Josie would have wanted details on her horse's death. He reminded himself they didn't know each other anymore, and he didn't know how to deal with this new Josie.

After a horse left or passed on, the nameplate was replaced most of the time. But for the special horses, the honorary nameplate remained. He didn't know why Big Joe had chosen to memorialize her horse this way, but as he watched the grief on Josie's face, he was glad he had.

Funny how he knew that she was upset without her having to shed a single tear. He could tell that seeing her old horse's stall, as much as she said she felt nothing, made her miss him.

Josie turned back to him. "I tried to bring him with me," she said. "But he refused. Leaving meant giving up everything I loved."

He hadn't known that. Then again, he'd only heard Joe's side of the story, because when Josie left, he'd been desperately trying to make a relationship work with a woman he couldn't stand but had to because she was carrying his baby.

"He always said that he had no idea what your plans were and that you just left without a word, just a note on the table," Brady said.

Josie shook her head.

"I'd been asking him for months about going to college. At that last show, where we had the big fight, a college scout was there and offered me the chance to go on scholarship. My father refused. That's what the fight was about."

Her expression changed to reveal the vulnerable girl he once knew who used to share all her hopes and dreams with him. "I did everything he wanted. You know how badly I wanted to go to college, but he could never get that through his head. I had an amazing opportunity, but rather than talking about it and working on a compromise, he…"

She trailed off, and the sadness on her face made him wish he could comfort her in some way. Obviously, the fight was about way more than anyone had ever thought. Once again, Brady wanted to kick himself for not looking deeper.

After a long moment where Josie appeared to compose herself, she said, "It's true that the morning I left, I left a note on the table. But we'd had multiple conversations where he'd refused to listen. Even after I left, I tried to talk to him. His position was either 'come home,' or 'I have nothing to say to you.' I tried. Maybe, as he said, it was just a bunch of excuses. I sincerely did want to work things out with him. I also wanted to go to college and make my own life."

All this, Brady had known about her. He'd just been so wrapped up in his own life at the time, he hadn't seen it. After she'd left, it had been easier not to question. Not to open that space in his heart that genuinely missed her.

She gestured around the barn. "I know I probably sound just as stubborn as him about all of this. But I am trying to do the right thing here. I just don't know what that is."

Another glimpse of the vulnerable young girl she'd been peeked out, and he wished there hadn't been so much bad history that he could take her in his arms the way he used to and tell her they would figure it out together.

He'd promised her that once, and he'd let her down.

Maybe he should have asked more questions back then, but he'd had a lot on his plate. A young kid of nineteen with a baby on the way, figuring out what he should do. Maddie didn't have a loving, supportive family like he did, so he'd stepped up. His family had insisted he do the right thing, as had Joe. He'd never loved Maddie, and that was the worst part of it all. One bad decision at a party, and his life had completely changed. There were a lot of decisions he could have made differently back then, but Kayla was his world, and he would do anything for that little girl of his. Okay, not so little anymore. She was a teenager, a beautiful young woman, and he would do anything for her.

Kayla loved the stables just as much as Brady had, and losing the stables would mean she'd have no way to interact with the horses she loved so much. Which was one more reason why he would do whatever it took to make sure Josie felt comfortable letting him run this place.

He couldn't fix what had happened between him and Josie all those years ago, but hopefully, he could regain enough of her trust to save what mattered most to him.

He gestured toward the rest of the barn. "Let me show you some of the other improvements we've made over the years."

Josie screwed up her face the way she used to when she was upset and needed to push through and pretend it didn't bother her so she could get on with whatever her father had wanted her to do. He hated knowing her this way. It would be so much easier if she was just a stranger he could convince with logic and facts and numbers. But there were so many emotions they both had to contend with. Hopefully, they could get past some of them, at least enough for the logic and facts to convince her.

He continued the stables tour, ending at Big Joe's office. The man might have been meticulous about everything else, but the mess inside was enough to make anyone run in fear.

"I'm sorry about the mess, but he never let anyone but himself in here," Brady said as he opened the door.

Josie just shrugged. "I never spent much time in his office."

But when she saw the stacks of papers, she took a step back. "He didn't used to be so careless with paperwork," Josie said. "He could have a receipt from twenty years ago at his fingertips in a moment's notice."

Brady grinned. "Still could until the day he died. I don't know how he did it, though."

Josie shrugged as she walked into the office. "It doesn't matter now. But we're going to have to go through and organize all of this."

She picked up a stack of folders. "Well, at least I know where he kept all the invoices from the farrier."

Then she chuckled. "From nineteen eighty-three.

"We can probably throw it all away," Josie continued. "It wouldn't be a bad idea to digitize as many records as possible, just in case. I don't suppose anyone ever convinced him to get a computer."

The lighthearted tone in her voice gave him hope that maybe they could find a way through this after all. Yes, there were difficult emotions, but they could also rediscover funny things to reminisce about. Hopefully, he could find enough of those ways to make her laugh and smile and remember all the good things that once were and still could be.

"With so much of the horse world being managed online, he grudgingly agreed to get a computer. That's in the main stable office. He still did everything on regular paper by hand and just had one of the staff deal with the 'computer nonsense,' as he called it."

He laughed, trying to take advantage of the lighter mood, but the stony expression had already returned to her face.

"I'll want access to all of that information as well," she said. "I need a full picture of the business."

Okay. Back to business. He could handle that, too. Whatever it took to make this work. "You're the owner. Everything is at your disposal. I'm happy to answer any questions or give any explanations."

She nodded as she walked around the desk, then sat in the big imposing chair, her small frame making it look even bigger. An unexpected wave of grief hit Brady square in the chest as he remembered Big Joe sitting in that chair, puffing on a cigar and complaining about rising hay prices. Such a mundane memory, and yet as Josie shifted in the chair, a hint of the cigar smell came toward him, and Brady wished that Big Joe was still here and that it hadn't taken his death to bring Josie home.

"Are you okay?" Josie asked. "I know it's awfully stuffy in here and smells like those nasty cigars he loved. We need to air this room out."

He used to think those same cigars were nasty, too. Funny how, when you miss the person, you even missed their vices. Okay, he missed Big Joe. They might have had their differences, but he had grown fond of the old man. But he couldn't tell her that. Instead, he coughed, trying to rid himself of the emotion.

Josie held up a ledger book. "I can't believe he still did everything by hand. This is going to take forever to sort through."

"Abigail used to try to get him to change every year at tax time, to move everything to the computer to make it easier on his accountant, but he never would."

Josie appeared to be studying the books thoroughly.

"Who handles all the accounts receivable?"

Brady shrugged. "He did. He handled it all. If he wasn't around and someone brought in payment, they just stuck it in the lockbox."

"What about the accounts that were in arrears?"

Brady shook his head. "I don't know anything about that. I mean, there were times when people would say they couldn't pay for the lesson, but I had them talk to Big Joe because he preferred to handle that personally."

"Well," she said, peering at the ledger pages. "You'd better hope that he just did a very bad job of writing down when people paid him because, by the looks of this, at least half of your customers haven't paid in months."

He sucked in a breath. He'd known that some of the families had fallen on hard times and knew that Big Joe would sometimes give them a break. But half? Surely that couldn't be right.

"Can I take a look?" he asked, coming over to her side of the desk. When she turned the ledger his way, his stomach sank. He knew all those names. Knew that it probably wasn't an accounting error. He wasn't a math genius by any stretch, but all it took was a glance to see that the stables were operating in the red and likely had been for some time. It would be hard enough to convince Josie not to sell a profitable business. But knowing just how bad things were financially, he wasn't sure how he would do it.

Now, that final conversation here in this office with Joe about the rising hay prices wasn't just some old guy griping because that's what old guys did, but the worries of a man whose business wasn't bringing in enough money.

A couple of days before he died, Joe hadn't been around to pay for the vet bill. Usually, the vet would tell him that he'd send the invoice, but he'd insisted on it being paid right then, saying that the policy had changed. At the time, Brady hadn't thought much of it and handed him his credit card, knowing that Big Joe would reimburse him. Was the change in policy more about Joe's tight finances? At this point, Brady wasn't going to say anything about the vet bill. It had only been a few hundred dollars, anyway, and it didn't seem worth the trouble.

Which was a good thing because the furrows in Josie's brow had deepened.

"I know I said I'd try to let you keep the stables open," Josie said, looking up at him. "But surely you can see why it's looking more and more like there's no way we can do that."

Her voice held enough of a sympathetic

tone that he believed this wasn't the conclusion she'd wanted to come to. The vet bill he'd paid wasn't a big deal, but looking at the numbers on the ledger in front of Josie, there was no way Brady could scrape together enough to even come close to paying those debts.

With so much stacked against him, how was he supposed to keep the stables open now?

Chapter Three

Josie had thought that the will had been her father's final revenge. But that was before she'd taken a look at the books. Though she asked Brady if her father could have made some mistakes in not entering payments, she knew better. He was too meticulous about counting every penny. He wouldn't have forgotten or made a mistake.

The stables were losing thousands of dollars every month. Nothing was paying for itself. Not the horse boarding, the group and individual riding lessons, the more complex training of animals and riders, or the community events they sometimes performed at. Unpaid invoices sat alongside unpaid bills. It was just a question of how far in the hole they were. She'd promised Abigail she'd find a way to keep it open, but looking at the pre-liminary numbers, she didn't see how. Josie didn't have the money to support it, and based on all of these customers who weren't pay-ing, no one here did, either. Her only option was likely going to be to sell. An unpaid bill for hay sat on top of the ledger. Fifteen thou-sand dollars and the income they had wasn't going to be enough to cover it. Josie closed the book, picked it up and stood.

"I don't think I have to explain in detail how dire the financial condition of the stables is. I will go through this tonight and see what I can find. But if you're serious about making this work, then I suggest you make a list of everything we can possibly sell here, as well as any nonessential staff that can be laid off."

Yes, she knew it was sacrilege even to sug-gest laying off loyal staff. But looking at the numbers, what her father paid out in wages alone was more than their income. Add in operating expenses and any other inciden-tals, and it was amazing they were even still open. Granted, if everyone who had promised to pay actually paid, it would be a different situation, but things would be tight even then.

While she knew that her father had always tried to keep fees low to make the riding program affordable for everyone, they were too low. For the families who used the stables, this was an amazing deal. One reason she hadn't gotten a horse in Denver was because of the astronomically high boarding fees. Here it was a steal. Why had her father even suggested spending the money to increase the available stalls when he wouldn't be charging enough to pay for it?

It was hard to breathe inside this disgusting, smoky room. Maybe some fresh air would help her think better.

Josie scooted past Brady, forgetting about her ankle. Twisting, she fell right into him.

"It's okay. I got you."

She wasn't supposed to like being in his arms. She'd done everything she could to maintain her distance from him. How could someone who'd broken her heart years ago make her still get all fluttery inside at the touch?

Josie quickly shifted to use the desk as a prop to hold herself up as she reached for her crutches.

"Thank you. I've got it now."

The expression on his face told her he thought she was a liar. Maybe she was. But she had fought too long and too hard to get over him to be feeling this way right now.

"Dad!"

The exact reason she had for not trusting him came bounding into the office.

"My lesson starts in ten minutes."

"Thanks, kiddo. I was helping Josie go through some of her father's things, and I lost track of time. Sorry. I'll be right there."

Brady reached for the ledger book that Josie struggled to hold as she maneuvered her crutches.

"Let me take that. I can carry it for you as far as the arena, and then, if you don't want to watch the ride, we'll see if someone can take it the rest of the way to the house for you. I hope you will stay and watch. Kayla is becoming quite the accomplished trick rider. Like someone else I used to know."

He winked at her like he was trying to form some kind of solidarity over the good old days. Except that they weren't the good old days for her. Josie had hated trick riding and had been terrified of most of the tricks her father had made her do. But whenever she admitted fear, her father would tell her that the only way to conquer her fear was to just do it—so she'd done it. When she no longer had to do it, she promised herself she'd never ride trick again.

Brady had known how scared she was, so it was funny to see the pride he had in his daughter doing it.

"I'm going to do the full stroud today," Kayla said excitedly, mentioning the trick where the rider hung off sideways and perpendicular from the side of the horse.

Brady beamed with pride. "That's great. That was Josie's best trick. Maybe she can watch and give you some tips."

The biggest tip would be "don't do it." Full stroud was a dangerous trick, and even the best riders had serious injuries. But that wasn't her call. She wasn't Kayla's parent, and while she did own the stables, Josie hadn't been part of this world for so long, it wasn't right for her to step in.

Kayla looked over at Josie with the same air of disdain that Maddie used to give her. "Why would I do that? My mom was the best."

Funny how Kayla had never even met Josie. It had been years since Maddie and Josie had spoken, and yet Maddie was still planting the seeds of hatred in her daughter. Even after all this time, the childhood rivalry was still there.

"Actually," Brady said, "your mom never

could quite get the full stroud right. Now, if we're talking death drag, your mom was amazing."

Brady spoke the truth. That was the silly thing about the competition Maddie had made up between the two of them. Maddie was a talented rider in her own right and had plenty of skills that Josie didn't. Rather than Maddie understanding that everyone had their own abilities and talents, she had made it a contest over everything.

"Your dad is right. Your mom had an amazing death drag. I've never seen anyone do it as well as she did."

Kayla merely stared at Josie.

Josie handed the ledger to Brady. "Thanks for the help. Why don't you hurry and get to the arena, and I'll catch up. You don't want to miss your daughter's ride."

Kayla smiled, then pranced out of the room, very much like Maddie used to do. So interesting to see how alike mother and daughter were.

Brady looked over at Josie as if he didn't want to leave her.

"Go," Josie said. "Neither of us will hear the end of it if you miss a second of your daughter's ride because of me. I'll be fine."

Brady nodded slowly, like he knew Josie was right but didn't like it. But it wasn't for him to like or not. His first responsibility was to his daughter, and even though Josie appreciated that he wanted to look out for Josie and keep her safe, being there for his daughter was more important.

She'd never disagreed with that point. Since Brady's role in Maddie's pregnancy was known, Josie had steered clear of them to give them a chance to be a family. Though there were times in the past when she would have liked to have talked to him, to find out why he would have cheated on her with Maddie, breaking the promise they made to each other, the answers hadn't been worth hurting a child. What difference would it have made even if they had talked things through? Brady needed to be there for his daughter.

By the time Josie got to the arena, the riding lesson was in full swing, and Maddie was there observing as well. Josie didn't need to watch for long to know that Kayla's form was terrible. She was going into the trick completely wrong, likely because she didn't have the abdominal strength to do it properly. That had been Maddie's problem, too. As much as Josie hated to admit it, the hours her father made her spend training were not all for nothing. It hadn't just been about the horses, but was also about her own physical condition and keeping her body in top shape. When all the girls like Maddie were out partying and having a good time with their friends, Josie was in the makeshift gym her father had put in the stables. What everyone thought was Josie's natural talent had been a lot of hard work.

"Put some muscle into it," Maddie screamed from the sidelines. "You're doing it wrong."

Josie turned to Abigail, who had come to stand beside her. "Are parents allowed to coach from the bleachers now?"

Abigail shook her head. "No. But try telling that to Maddie."

Josie shouldn't get involved. This was none of her business. But from where she stood, she could see the tears of frustration running down the girl's cheeks. Her father would remove any parent from the stands for yelling at their kid like that back in the day. Not that he disapproved of yelling at one's child, but it was a distraction from the teachers giving instructions, and therefore a safety hazard. Listening to her mom scream at her was something Kayla didn't need when attempting an extremely dangerous trick.

"Put your back into it," Maddie yelled.

It was the least helpful thing anyone could say to her. This was all abs. Using her back muscles could hurt her. This was why the instructions needed to come from the instructor, not someone on the sidelines.

Mike Fry, the trainer handling the group lesson today, seemed to have the same opinion, as he strolled over to the side of the fence and said something to Maddie. She looked like she was arguing with him for a moment, then Mike shook his head and walked away.

None of Josie's business.

And yet, it was. Technically, Josie was the owner of the stables now, and if Kayla got hurt because of such an obvious safety violation, it was on Josie.

Josie turned to Abigail. "Come with me."

Though Josie had been gone a long time, the expression on Abigail's face said she knew exactly what Josie was going to do, and she wasn't sure if she liked it.

Josie hobbled over to Maddie.

"If I hear you yell at her one more time, I will have you removed from the stands."

Kayla was attempting another trick, the

slick stand, and as soon as Kayla got up, Josie knew she wasn't going to stay up for very long.

As the girl wobbled, Maddie yelled, "Watch your posture."

At that moment Kayla turned to look at her mother, and in doing so, she slipped and fell.

Kayla immediately got up and brushed the dirt off her, and it was obvious she wasn't hurt. Unless you counted her pride. More tears rolled down the girl's cheeks. Josie turned her attention back to Maddie.

"Leave the stands now."

Josie turned to Abigail for backup, but Abigail had already gone and grabbed Brady.

"What's going on here?" Brady asked.

"Maddie knows the rules. No coaching from the sidelines. She just yelled at Kayla and distracted her, and she fell. I will not have this kind of safety violation here—not now, not with so much at stake."

Brady hesitated slightly.

"If this were any other parent, you would have asked them to leave by now," Josie said.

Brady took off his hat and ran his hand through his hair before setting his hat back on.

"Maddie, you know the rules. I try to keep

these conversations private between us, but you're leaving me no choice. Please go wait in your truck until Kayla's lesson is over."

"Of course you're taking her side," Maddie snapped. "This wasn't a problem when Big Joe was alive."

Brady made an exasperated noise. "That's not true, and you know it. This isn't the first time we've had this conversation. Don't blame Josie for your actions."

This was why Josie had avoided Brady and Maddie once Maddie's pregnancy was known. Maddie's jealousy of Josie had always gotten in the way of reason, and it wasn't fair to put a child in the middle of it. Even now, when Kayla's safety was at stake, Maddie's irrational refusal to see facts was getting in the way.

How was Josie supposed to work with Brady on finding a way to keep the stables open when Maddie took the enforcement of a safety rule personally?

Maddie glared at Josie. "You're just trying to get even with me for stealing your boyfriend."

At least they were getting this out in the open now.

As Maddie stomped off to the parking lot,

Josie took a deep breath. She should probably give Maddie time to cool off, but she wanted to clear the air.

Josie followed Maddie to the parking lot, Brady and Abigail on her heels.

"Maddie, hold up a minute," Josie said when she caught up to her. "We need to get something straight. This is about the safety of your child. I gave up on Brady the second he confirmed you were having his baby. Kayla is the most important thing here. She's completely innocent in this situation. Putting her first is the right thing to do."

She glanced at Brady, then at Maddie. "I'm sorry for all the things that happened in the past. I apologize for everything I've ever said or done wrong, and I forgive you for everything you said or did to me. Can we please let go of the past so we can focus on the future?"

Abigail came up to Josie and put her arm around her. Josie had done her best to pretend she wasn't hurt when everything went down, but Abigail had known. She'd done everything she could to make Josie feel better, to make her life easier during that time.

Maybe the forgiveness speech Josie had just given Maddie was something Josie needed to take to heart as well. Her father was dead. She couldn't keep holding his misdeeds in her heart, preventing her from moving forward with the future. Which meant she also had to let go of her weird feelings about Brady. Yes, Brady had broken her heart, but they were different people now. Working with him meant letting go of their past.

Like it or not, her father had given her a nearly bankrupt stable to run, presumably with Brady. While Josie wanted nothing more than to wash her hands of the place, Abigail's warm presence reminded her that people she loved were counting on her to put her personal feelings aside for their sakes.

Except Maddie wasn't in a forgiving mood. "We all know your agenda, so I know this isn't about what's best for Kayla. You'll do whatever you can to destroy this place, and I'm going to stop you."

"My plans have changed," Josie said. "Abigail reminded me that there is something here worth trying to save. I don't know if I can do it or not, but Brady has promised to help me try."

Brady's attention was on the arena, where Kayla was getting ready to do another trick.

"We'll get there," Brady said, not taking his eyes off his daughter. "It's going to take a lot of work, but I have faith."

The squeeze Abigail gave her made Josie feel better. This was why she was doing it. Regardless of what anyone else thought, she had to stay focused on making things right with the person who'd always done right by Josie.

"Kayla looks really good," Josie said, trying to focus her attention back on the arena.

Even without being in the direct line of Maddie's glare, Josie could feel its sting.

"Don't butter me up," Maddie said. "I know her strengths and weaknesses, and I'm sure you have plenty of criticism on her form."

Kayla completed the trick and got back into line as the next girl started her trick. Preparing herself for the expression of death Josie had hated as a teen, she turned her full attention on Maddie.

"I meant my compliment sincerely. You don't know me anymore. Just like I don't know you."

Though Josie had just told herself that she needed to let go of the past, the words of her old youth pastor came to mind.

"Maybe you should give Maddie a break," he'd said. "You girls are always at each other's throats, but you never stop to look at things from the other side. Get to know her. I think you'll have more in common with her than you think."

They'd been forced to share a bunk at youth camp, and Maddie had done everything she could to make Josie miserable. At the time, Josie had found it incredibly unfair that Lee was taking Maddie's side, even though Maddie had started it all. But, in wanting to do the right thing and thinking that doing the right thing was the way to please God, Josie had tried to be nice to Maddie, only to be met with more insults and nastiness.

Just like now.

These days, Josie wasn't sure what role God played in her life. She still believed in Him, but she didn't know what that meant anymore. She wasn't so blind, though, that she didn't see that God wanted her to do something here.

Though Brady and Maddie weren't a couple, Maddie was the mother of his daughter and the parent of one of their riders. For the sake of the stables, Josie had to find a way to get along. The only difference between this and the difficult parents in Josie's programs was the personal connection here.

None of this was what Josie wanted. With the bleak financial outlook of the stables, she could easily sell and walk away. She didn't have to deal with these emotions or her difficult past. And she really didn't have to work with the only man who'd ever gotten close enough to her heart to break it.

But, between the love of her cousin, and these reminders that maybe God had a plan, Josie had to do what she could to make things right.

Josie took a deep breath before addressing Maddie. "The truth is, we never really did get to know each other. We were too busy hating each other, for some reason I've never understood. I want to do right by the stables, which means doing right by your daughter. Can we find a way to work through this?"

Brady had never been so proud of Josie in his life. He'd been there for her wins in the arena, and he'd seen her strength of character many times before. But in the past, when Maddie picked on her, Josie would usually say nothing, then later, he'd find her crying. She used to always pretend that Maddie never hurt her, but Brady had known. Sometimes he thought that Maddie always escalated the trouble between them to get a reaction. But Josie never would. At least not in front of others. Not even when Maddie had very publicly announced that she was carrying his baby. Josie had just stood there, stoically, and it wasn't until later that she had broken down.

Not that Brady had witnessed the breakdown. Josie had privately asked him, very quietly, if it was true, and when he'd confirmed, she had simply nodded and said, "I wish you the best," and that was the last thing she'd ever said to him until she'd come back here.

Maddie was the one making things difficult by bringing up the past. He could tell that Josie was doing her best to move on, and she didn't have to.

By all rights, Josie was the wounded party. But she was trying to put aside those wounds and move forward.

Seeing this strong, beautiful woman working so hard to do the right thing made him admire her all the more. There was still so much of the woman he'd once loved inside her, and he wished he hadn't messed things up between them.

Of all people to get pregnant, why did it have to be Maddie? He'd asked God that a thousand times over the years, and the best thing he could tell was that it was intended for him to be able to show grace to someone who didn't deserve it. Just like Josie was doing now.

"Leopards don't change their spots," Maddie said. "I know the kind of person you really are and how all of this is fake. Do what you're going to do, and then go home and leave the rest of us in peace."

Brady stepped forward. "That's enough. Why can't you take it in good faith that Josie is trying here? You always go back to the idea of the kind of person she really is, but you've never offered proof."

Even in the short time Josie had been back, he'd seen Josie's struggle to do the right thing, despite her pain. They may not know each other anymore, but her character hadn't changed. She was still a woman he deeply admired. He took a deep breath, hoping not to have an argument with Maddie, especially since Kayla would be having her turn again in a few minutes.

Though he'd seen Maddie's anger at Josie at the will reading, he hadn't considered until now that she might make working with Josie difficult. Not that Maddie had any claim on him, other than as a partner in raising their daughter, but he worked hard to try to get along with her, so she needed to let go of her grudge against Josie.

"Besides, Josie is right," Brady said. "None of us are the same people we were all those years ago. We've all grown and changed. Can't we just put the past behind us and start over?"

The expression that flashed across Josie's face surprised him. He had thought she'd appreciate him agreeing with her about putting the past in the past, but if he knew anything from the time they'd spent together, he'd touched on a wound.

Josie might say she was willing to move forward, but it was foolish to think it would be easy. He'd hurt her, but it would take time for him to regain her trust. Working together was going to be easier said than done.

"Whatever," Maddie said. "You've always taken her side."

Maddie stomped off to the truck, but he didn't follow her. He didn't want to have these fights with her. He did everything he could to get along, even if it meant swallowing his pride time and again for the sake of the child they shared. He turned his attention back to the arena, where Kayla was getting ready to take another turn. The slick stand, from which she'd fallen just a little bit earlier. But this time, she managed it perfectly, and he didn't have to look over at Josie to know she was smiling. Strange how he could still sense these things about her after so much time apart.

"She looks really good," Josie said. "You should be proud of her."

"I am. She's been working hard."

Abigail turned to him. "My co-instructor is on the other side of the arena, and we were going to go over what we were doing in class today. Can you stay here for a few minutes to help Josie?"

"I'll be fine," Josie said, but he nodded at Abigail and caught her knowing look. Josie always said she'd be fine, so it meant they had to work harder at making sure of it.

Abigail headed off, leaving them to watch the rest of the ride. As he watched Sam, the next girl, do her trick, he remembered how Josie had done the same one at a Cattlemen's Association banquet the summer before their lives had fallen apart. It had been the best summer of his life. They'd traveled to so many different shows and competitions, and their bond had grown.

After Josie left, they hadn't had as many

shows. Big Joe's cronies had privately told him that Big Joe's heart wasn't in it without his little girl. Nowadays, they only had a couple, and Big Joe had resisted Brady's efforts to find more.

"Hey, Josie?"

Josie turned away from the arena to look at him. "What?"

"You wanted to look at ways to save money. But what if we found ways to earn money?"

She nodded. "For sure. Based on what stables in Denver charge, people here are getting a great deal. We could definitely raise the rates, though if people are as bad off financially as you say, it might be difficult for them to pay. As it is, not everyone is paying."

At least she was still thinking along the lines of saving the place.

"That's not where I was going with this," he said. "Back when we were kids, we did a lot of shows. We don't do many anymore, so what if we put on a fundraiser show? A benefit to raise money, so we don't have to make as many cuts."

She looked at him like he'd just told her to take a dip in the water trough, then roll in a pile of manure.

"Your father had me running most of the

shows. I know what I'm doing. And, without him breathing down my neck, I could do something special."

As he spoke, he thought of everything he could do to improve their show. Big Joe wouldn't listen to his suggestions in the past, but now, he'd have full control.

"It takes a lot to put on a show," Josie said, her voice lacking any sign of encouragement. "Even though it's to raise money, there's a lot of initial outlay. I put on lots of events with my job as well."

She started ticking off a list of all the things they'd need to put on the event. From that perspective, it did sound hopeless. But many of the things she mentioned, he knew they could get for free from community members if they just asked. That was the difference between here and the city.

"We'll have it here at the indoor arena. We can get volunteers to do cleanup, maintenance, setup, all that. I'm sure we can get supplies donated by our local businesses. No one wants to see this place sold. If we say it's to save the stables, we'll get even more interest."

Josie sighed. "And if it's not enough to save the stables?"

He hadn't thought of that.

"It's better than not trying," he finally said.

She looked like she was about to cry, but then turned away. In the past, he'd have been able to give her some comfort, or at least ask what was on her mind that she found so upsetting.

Not that he needed much of an explanation. She'd had to come back to clean up a mess she didn't make in a place she didn't want to be. For him, the shows had been full of positive memories. But he'd seen enough of her tears to know they were more bitter than sweet.

"I'm sorry to put you in this position," he said quietly.

She didn't turn, but she shook her head softly. "You didn't. He did."

Her voice shook slightly, as if she was crying or about to. Her father had not abused her, but he'd been authoritarian when it came to his expectations. He'd pushed her hard to excel, and when she did, he never said a word of praise. He was quick with criticism, though, and then his words were sharp, almost cruel.

When Brady took a step toward her, she shook her head again.

"Don't. I know you mean well, but my father wasn't the only one who hurt me. And while I'm trying to work on moving past it, it's not that easy."

His gut ached. She'd finally said it. It wasn't like it was a secret that he'd hurt her. But this was the first she'd admitted it to him like this.

Kayla's trick class ended and the riders filed out. Kayla was laughing with a group of friends, oblivious to him. He'd been worried that the situation with her mom would have upset her, but she seemed in a good place, so he let her be. Which was a relief because he didn't know what to do about Josie.

Fortunately, he didn't have to say more as Abigail returned. As soon as she saw the expression on Josie's face, she glared at him.

"I can't leave you two alone for ten minutes?"

Josie shook her head. "It's fine. Just me dealing with stuff. I don't know why I have to be so emotional."

He knew. She'd never been taught how to handle her emotions in a healthy way. He might not have had the opportunity to go to college, but working with the kids, he'd read everything he could get his hands on to help their psychological development. Big Joe had snorted and said it was a waste of Brady's time, but Brady had learned a lot of good things.

A little girl ran up to them and wrapped her arms around Abigail. "Miss Abigail! I got an A on my spelling test!"

Abigail hugged the little girl back. "Great! You get to lead warm-ups today. Now go get ready."

As the little girl ran off, Abigail smiled at them. "She's been struggling in school, so I've been giving her incentives at the arena if she does well with her studies."

Then Abigail turned her attention to Josie. "So what did you think? Did you get a chance to take stock of everything, or is there anything else we can show you to make a decision?"

Wow. Bad timing. He'd hoped to at least have had a chance to get Josie to think about things before springing this on her.

Before he could think of a response, Josie said, "I'll be honest. It doesn't look good. This place is in terrible shape financially, and I don't have the means to make it work."

"But we have a waiting list," Abigail said. "How is that possible?"

Josie turned, so she was facing them all. "I

don't know. But you're welcome to join me in going through the books to figure it out."

She gestured at the ledger book sitting on the bleachers. Then she turned her attention to him, an expression of deep pain on her face.

"Brady would like to host a benefit show to raise the needed funds to keep the stables open. I don't know if it will be enough to get us in the black, but if you want to do this, then I'll let you try."

She was putting the decision on Abigail. Brady didn't have to talk to her to know that her answer would be yes. Abigail used to go with him to talk to Big Joe about doing more shows.

Abigail reached over and touched Josie's arm. "But what do you want? What about your job and your life back in Denver?"

He hadn't been expecting that. But as he saw the glances exchanged by the women, he understood. They were both trying to do the right thing for each other, even though it went against their own personal interests. Josie might have been gone, but the love the two shared had only strengthened with time.

"I have to be back to work on Monday," Josie said. "I can come on weekends, and I have some vacation I can use, but I'll need some time to sort out coverage while I'm gone."

Brady blew out a breath. Maybe it wasn't a solution, but it was progress.

"Are you sure?" Abigail asked.

Josie gestured at the little girl standing in line to get her horse. "That's your world. You have loved me the best of anyone in my life. I have to do this for you."

"You don't," Abigail said.

Josie squared her shoulders like she always did when her mind was made up, and she was being stubborn. "I want to."

He wanted to hug Josie right now, but he couldn't. Instead, he said a silent prayer of thanks that they were being given a chance.

No, they weren't out of the woods yet. But they had hope. And for now, hope was enough.

Chapter Four

Maybe she'd been overconfident in thinking that because she ran a much larger program for her day job that she could do this as well. Josie stared at the unpaid invoices in front of her and sighed. A month after inheriting the stables, Josie still wasn't sure where they would get the money. None of this fit with the man she'd known her father to be. She could remember his cronies joking that Big Joe could squeeze a penny so hard it would turn into a dime just to relieve the pressure.

Brady stepped into the office, looking as worn-out as she felt.

"I thought you were taking the day off," she said. "Weren't you going to spend the day with Kayla?"

Slumping into a chair, Brady sighed. "Maddie decided to have a girls' day with her. I can't compete with a spa day and shopping."

He ran his hand down his face, looking despondent. "What happened to the days when coming with Dad to feed the livestock was considered fun?"

Josie laughed. "Those days end when the teenage years begin. I would have given anything to have had a mom to do those things with."

"You had Abigail." Brady looked up at her like he didn't understand.

"Abigail was great," Josie admitted. "She did her best, but she wasn't my mom. I know I didn't appreciate her the way I should have back then, but she was never equipped to be a parent. She was just a child herself, and she never asked to be in that position. Regardless, it's not the same as a mother-daughter relationship."

The pained expression on Brady's face made her realize this wasn't about a mother-daughter relationship, but his relationship as a father to his daughter. Josie wasn't an expert on that, either.

But maybe she could ease his troubled mind. "For what it's worth, it's clear Kayla adores you. She might prefer a spa day with her mom today, but the expression on her face when she's with you tells me that she's always going to need her dad."

The way his eyes brightened when he looked up at her reminded Josie of the good old days. They used to know all the right things to say to each other, to give the encouragement needed. Funny how easily they fell back into that pattern, even though so much time had passed.

Unfortunately, too many other things had passed between them ever to return to those days. So she resisted the urge to hug him as he smiled.

"You're right," he said. "I'm just being sentimental. They grow up way too fast. Though I thank God every day for every moment I'm given, it still feels like not enough."

When he made comments like that, it reminded Josie of two things—one, why she'd loved him to begin with, and two, that he'd been right to stand by Maddie, even if it meant breaking Josie's heart. A hard paradox to live with since they were going to be working so closely together, and it was difficult not to like him again. Could she overlook the fact that he'd broken the most important promises he'd made to her? And was it safe for her to do so?

Brady stood and gestured at the stack of invoices she'd been staring at. "Did you make any headway?"

Right. The way out was to focus on the business at hand, not dwell on the past. It had been so much easier to remain in the present when she'd been far removed from this place.

She handed him the hay bill. "This is my biggest concern. Not only do we not have enough money to pay it, but our current supply is dwindling, and to get another delivery, we have to pay this bill, plus pay for that delivery. I'm not sure how we can keep the animals fed."

"I have the same concern," he admitted. "Big Joe was upset about rising hay prices, but when I offered to shop around, he told me that he'd always done business with the Hendersons, and he wasn't about to change that."

That was always how her father had done things. "I did a quick search online, and he's been paying nearly double the rate of others. Is their hay special in some way?"

Brady shook his head. "Two-thirds of what we get is standard grass hay, and the rest is alfalfa. But you can get that anywhere. There's no reason it should be double the price. Sure, there are some fluctuations in price and quality, but not to that degree."

She could almost hear her father arguing that loyalty meant everything in this business, which she could appreciate. Still, his stubborn insistence on remaining with a more expensive supplier made it hard to keep the stables open.

"Can you dig deeper on this?" Josie asked. "Find out what it'll cost to switch to another provider, and also talk to the Hendersons to see what they can do about the bill. I know they have to provide for their family as well, but I'm not sure how they can justify such a high price."

She caught the smirk on Brady's face just as he turned his head.

"What? You clearly have something to say but don't want to say it. If we're going to make this work, you're going to have to be straight with me."

Whatever he'd been holding in, he let out in a big laugh. "I've missed this."

"Missed what? We're dealing with a financial crisis, and you're laughing at me?"

He shrugged. "There's just this way about you. Once you set your mind to something, you charge full steam ahead. I know you didn't want the stables, but here you are, already taking ownership. You do the hard things you don't want to do for the benefit of others. I've always loved that about you."

A lump caught in her throat at his words. What was she supposed to say? She'd been the one to ask, and now she had to sit with the uncomfortable truth. He'd always seen the good in her, even when she felt as worthless as a toad. It was no secret she didn't want to be here, but somehow, he made it seem like she was a much better person than she was.

She cleared her throat. Enough of this emotional stuff. He'd made his choice long ago. He might have seen her as a better person than she'd thought she was, but it still hadn't been good enough to keep him. Rather, he'd preferred to be with her worst enemy.

"Anyway," she said, "I would appreciate you taking care of the hay situation. I'm going to look into these other bills. Abigail has been helping me go through the list of people who owe us money, and we can see what we can try to collect on."

Brady made a noise like he wanted to argue with her, but then he nodded. He'd likely realized he'd said too much. They couldn't dwell on things from the past, like what they'd admired about each other.

But no amount of therapy, no prayers to a God who never answered her and none of the books she'd read had prepared her for this. Her father was dead and gone, but everything around her was a constant reminder of him.

Why couldn't he have loved her?

She'd asked that question millions of times with no answer.

And, if she was honest, she didn't know if she meant her father or Brady.

Enough.

She grabbed the nearest file, not caring what it was for.

"I'm going to go outside and look through this. It's too stuffy in here," she said.

Abigail had come in and cleaned after Josie had commented on the smell. But the stench of cigars permeated everything in the room. The ledgers she'd brought to the house had made her room stink, so she'd had to take them into another room. It would be nice to get home, where she could breathe again.

"You don't have to leave," Brady said. "I'll go."

He hesitated slightly, then said, "Look, I'm sorry if I made things weird between us by bringing up our past. It's hard, seeing you now, and remembering what we were."

Didn't she know it?

"I'm not the one who broke things between us."

There. She said it—the thing she'd wanted to say for so long but couldn't. The only question missing was "Why?" but she wasn't sure she could handle the answer.

Brady nodded slowly. "I know. I just need you to understand that I never meant to hurt you. Losing you was the hardest thing I'd ever had to do."

Josie slammed the folder back down on the desk. "Never meant to hurt me? I'm tired of dancing around this. It's fine that you chose to be a father. I support that decision one hundred percent. But the part you ignore is that you cheated in the first place. The decision to cheat? That's how you lost me."

If she was going to move past whatever this was with Brady, he needed to know that his nobility wasn't what had hurt things between them. It was his betrayal.

"I know." He hung his head. "I used to think a lot about what I'd tell you if you ever asked for an explanation."

"I'm not asking for one," she said, crossing

her arms across her chest. "But I can't pretend anymore that you didn't hurt me, and you have to stop pretending as well."

This time, Brady nodded. "You're right. There isn't an adequate apology for what I did to you. I am sorry. I wish I could give you more than that."

He looked legitimately distraught, but it didn't make her feel any better.

Josie glanced at the folder she'd set down. Programs from previous shows.

"This could be useful for our benefit planning. How much of the original schedule would still work?" She handed it to him, hoping that focusing back on work would help calm the tumultuous emotions inside her.

He studied the documents. "We don't have all the same acts, but there's a lot we can do."

Moving closer to her, he held out one of the programs. "Do you remember this show in Texas? That was a fun trip."

More memories she didn't want to deal with. Yes, it had been a fun trip. As they'd passed several ranches on the long drive, they'd talked about the future and the kind of ranch they someday hoped to own together. So many broken dreams.

"I don't know how we're supposed to keep

doing this," she finally said. "I know it's been fifteen years, but it feels like yesterday."

The expression on his face was as heavy as her heart felt. "It's probably not my place to ask, but have you gone to the Lord with this? I'm not making excuses for myself, but it seems like you've been holding on to a lot of hurt for a long time, hurt I can't make go away no matter what I do or say."

Now he sounded like her therapist. Let it go. That's what everyone told her. And she thought she had. Until she had to come back here. Josie had been doing just fine until she'd been forced to return.

"I don't pray anymore," she said quietly.

Brady stared at her. "What do you mean, you don't pray anymore? You used to be one of the leaders in our youth group. You were one of the reasons for my strong faith."

"And look at the good it did me!" Her heart thudded in her chest, and her throat ached from tears that wanted to come, but she wasn't going to let them. "I did everything right. Whatever my father asked of me, I did it. He still found fault with me. I kept my relationship with you pure and honoring God, and you chose to break your vows with my worst enemy. I prayed every day for blessings that never came, and I finally had enough."

Josie swallowed, then straightened. "My life got better when I finally started living it on my terms. Not trying to be good for my father, or God, or even you. I no longer have to perform for anyone."

Funny, those words were supposed to make her feel better, to remind her of her strength. Instead, she only wanted to cry even more.

"God has never asked anyone to perform. He just wants you to love Him. And if you think that I loved you based on your performance, then you never really knew me at all."

She looked him straight in the eye. "If I had been good enough for you, and you had loved me, you wouldn't have cheated."

Brady bent slightly, as if she'd given him a literal punch in the gut, then he shook his head slowly as he straightened again. "That's not what happened. I got drunk at a party. The drinks were so good, I didn't realize how much alcohol they had. I don't remember most of the night or why I made the choices I made. I just remember waking up feeling terrible, not knowing what had happened and feeling like I had failed you. It was never about you not being good enough, but about how I had proved myself unworthy."

His eyes were getting red and misty, like he was trying not to cry. Josie's insides ached. This was the most she'd heard about his side of the story. At first, she'd refused to talk to him because she'd seen the pictures of him in Maddie's arms. Then, when news of Maddie's pregnancy came out, it was too late. Brady had chosen the baby, and rightfully so.

None of this changed things.

"I did everything right," she said. "Maybe if I had gone that night—"

"No." Brady let out a long sigh. "You did the right thing in not going. I was dumb and gave in to peer pressure from Kyle Rawlins and went, even though I promised you I'd stay home."

It was hard to hear how Josie had lost her faith. A part of him had always hoped that someday he and Josie would find their way back together. But he had been foolish. Josie wasn't the same person he once loved. He didn't recognize this woman anymore. The Josie he'd loved had an unrelenting faith and deep belief that God's love would get her through just about anything.

"For a long time, I believed that God was punishing me for my mistake with Maddie. But Bible study, prayer and spending time with other believers has shown me that despite all my mistakes, God has chosen to richly bless me, and He loves me, no matter what."

He straightened, then looked at her earnestly. "Your faith always inspired me to seek the Lord more deeply. I'm sorry if my sins shook it. I wish with all my heart you would try to believe again and not let one tragedy ruin your relationship with God."

He went back to studying the programs Josie had shown him. They represented a lot of good memories and would give them ideas on building a stronger future for the stables... if only Josie could get past her hurt.

"It wasn't just one tragedy," she said slowly. "It was the sum of everything I'd been through, and that was the straw that broke the camel's back. I'd done everything right, and none of it mattered."

The pain in her eyes made him wish there was some way he could take it from her. But this was between her and God.

"That's not how faith works," he told her. "It's not a transactional thing, where you give

God your devotion in exchange for what you want. You taught me that."

Did she remember that time at the show in Wyoming, when he'd expressed frustration that for all his prayers, his horse still was acting up? How many times had she told him that God wasn't a short-order cook to serve what you want, but someone who wanted to know him? Brady wouldn't know Christ in such a profound way had it not been for all those talks he'd had with Josie.

Josie nodded slowly. "It feels like a lifetime ago. I put it all behind me."

"Have you?" He examined her face. She might have lost her faith, but he still knew how to read her. "You're holding on to so much unforgiveness. You say you put it behind you, but all the things you're upset about from the past are still holding you back."

Though he half expected her to argue or change the subject, she looked thoughtful for a moment. "I thought I'd dealt with everything, but I guess I just buried it."

A glimmer of the old Josie shone in her eyes.

"Will you consider going to church with me on Sunday?"

The expression on her face told him he'd

pushed too hard. But he wouldn't have felt right not asking her.

"I'm not sure I'm ready for that."

She gestured at the programs they'd been looking at. "This is hard enough for me as it is. I know we need to sort through these documents, not only to find ways of saving the stables, but also to plan the show. Dealing with all of this at once is more difficult than anyone gives me credit for."

Brady took a deep breath. "Since you've been back, you've mentioned all the things you hated about this place. All the wounds. Maybe, if you were reminded of the good things, you'd find it easier."

He held up the programs they'd been looking at, then pulled up the one for a fair in a small town in New Mexico they'd performed at. "Do you remember what a mess this show was? You and Betsy Rivers sat down and wrote out what you thought would be a better lineup and you said that if you ever ran a show of your own, you'd use that. Here you are, with the opportunity to do better, and you're so focused on how badly you've been hurt that you're not taking advantage of it."

Her sharp intake of breath told him he'd touched a nerve. Good. Big Joe hadn't been the best father. He was one of those old-school cowboys who'd thought the best way to love a child was to toughen them up. Brady had seen how it had affected Josie, and he'd tried to do better with Kayla.

That was the lesson he'd learned from the past. How to do better.

She took the paper out of his hand. "This lineup was so ridiculous. None of us had adequate time to change, let alone get some water. If we moved a couple things around, it would be so much better."

"Show me," he said.

Josie grabbed a stray legal pad from the desk and began writing out her ideal lineup, starting with the main act and working in smaller acts, like trick roping, whips and batons, in between to give riders time for costume changes, as well as giving the horses a break from riding complicated drills and performing various tricks.

"Also, we need to think about more practical costumes. We have zero budget for anything new, and I have no idea who can make them, but so many of the things my father had us wearing were hard to get in and out of and, frankly, didn't give us the right range of motion."

Maybe his pep talk had done some good after all. He was seeing the old Josie in action.

"Let's take a look at what we have in the costume room."

That was the one place they hadn't inventoried together yet.

They walked to the costume room, a bit faster than they'd been going, since Josie had graduated from crutches to a boot, and Brady pulled out the key to unlock it. By the dust covering every surface, he didn't think anyone had been in here since their last show over a year ago. He hadn't told Josie it had been that long, but over the last few years, they'd done fewer and fewer of them. Brady had tried to get Big Joe to do more, but he'd always brushed him off.

"Wow, it looks almost the same," Josie said as she walked in and ran her finger over one of the dusty tables. "Mrs. Fredrickson would have a fit if she could see this. She ran a tighter ship than my father."

Brady laughed as he remembered. "Her mission was to preserve the costumes at all costs."

It was good, having Josie laugh with him again. He'd always loved her laugh, and hearing it now gave him a new level of hope.

Today had made it clear that they could never get back to where they were. But a part of him wondered if there was a way they could find something again. Josie was a beautiful, intelligent woman with a big heart. He also wondered if God had brought them back together so he could help Josie rediscover her faith. She'd said that he didn't understand how difficult this was for her, facing so much at once. But he did know. And he admired her for it.

Josie pulled back the plastic covering a rack of garments. "Oh, wow! The stars-and-stripes costumes! Do you remember these?"

Brady went to her and pulled out one of the boys' shirts. "Yes. I don't know what they were made of, but it felt like they were covered in itching powder. It was terrible, trying to ride while wanting to scratch."

They laughed once more, and this was what Brady hoped they could find again. He'd never known anyone who laughed with him the way she did.

"We'd need a lot of help with the costumes," Josie said. "Is Mrs. Fredrickson still around?"

Brady shook his head. "She passed away a few years ago."

Josie's face darkened slightly, and he recognized the grief in her expression. "I might have joked about her, but she was a good woman. I'm sorry to hear she's gone."

Her face softened some more, and he felt the tension in the room ease.

"I do think about the people in this community from time to time. How they are, what they're up to. There were a lot of good people here."

"Still are," he said. "Even if you're not open to talking to God just yet, there are a lot of people at church who care about you and would love to see you again."

Josie nodded. "It was good to see everyone at the will reading, but it was so uncomfortable. Not the best circumstance for a catch-up, and I didn't seem to be anyone's favorite person."

Brady took a deep breath, hoping that God would give him the right words. It was true that there were a lot of hard feelings because she had so rashly insisted she didn't want the stables. Despite the bad blood between Josie and her father, Big Joe had not spoken against her, except about his disappointment in her leaving. Just prior to his death, Big Joe had mostly spoken of Josie in wistful terms, like he wanted her to come back but didn't know how to approach her. He couldn't tell Josie because she wasn't ready to hear that maybe her father wasn't all bad. As for the others, like him, they simply missed her.

"They were afraid you were going to sell the stables. But now that you're committed to helping save them, I think you'll be pleasantly surprised at how happy and eager to see you everyone would be."

Josie shrugged. "Maybe. But I haven't decided fully what I'm going to do."

She gestured at the dusty room, looking lost. "This is all so overwhelming, and honestly, I'm not sure the stables can be saved."

The Josie he remembered had always had a spirit of optimism, that they could conquer anything, achieve all their dreams. He almost didn't recognize this version of her, but as he remembered her confession about her lack of faith, he could understand why.

If one believed in God and had a deep love and understanding of His greatness, it was easy to also believe all things were possible. But not having that faith, not fully seeing the greatness of God's power and abilities, it was easy to give up in the face of what seemed like insurmountable obstacles.

"What about the benefit? You gave some

great ideas for the show lineup, and we're looking at possibilities for costumes. It's coming together. You might not be ready to go to church, but you know that's where all our supporters have always been. If they see that you're committed to trying to save the stables, and you're putting all your effort into this benefit, you're going to find the support you need."

The defeated look on her face made him wish they were back in the old days, when he could hug her and reassure her that things would work out. That had always been enough to perk her up, and she would charge forward with the enthusiasm of someone who believed they were limitless.

"We haven't even talked about what I'm working on," Brady said.

He pulled out the small notebook he always kept in his back pocket and flipped to the page where he had been taking notes while waiting for the water to fill when he watered the horses.

"I figure we can put on a show in about three months. That will give us time to create a lineup of the various acts and things the kids can do. That also gives us enough time to advertise the show. I'm going to invite some of my contacts in the rodeo world to use this as an audition to perform at their rodeos. Cash owes me a few favors, and I'm going to call him to see who else he can get here."

Josie's head jerked up at the mention of Cash. "Laura's husband?"

Brady nodded. "Yes. Despite his falling-out with Big Joe, we've still stayed in touch. He's been a good friend to me, and I know he'll help."

His response only made Josie look more downcast. "You forget that he's married to my cousin. She hates my father for not support-ing her marriage, and to be honest, I think I burned that bridge with her when I wouldn't go to her wedding."

It wasn't just the fact that Josie was so pes-simistic about everything, but it was the res-ignation in her voice at the idea that things couldn't improve.

"Have you tried reaching out to Laura? It's been almost ten years since they got married, so maybe she could forgive you for not going to her wedding."

He'd heard from Cash that Laura had been deeply hurt that not only had Josie refused to attend the wedding, but she also didn't stand up for her cousin as a bridesmaid. Back then,

Laura had hoped that her marriage would be an opportunity for the cousins to reestablish a relationship and maybe bring healing with Big Joe. But that was before Big Joe had declared Cash a worthless cowboy and refused to sanction a wedding between him and Laura.

"Maybe. I called her shortly after her wedding, but she hung up on me, saying it was too little, too late. The next few times I reached out, she wouldn't even talk to me. I gave up after that."

Josie let out a long sigh, then looked up at him. "The truth is, I couldn't go to her wedding because I knew you were Cash's best man. I didn't want to face you. I'd just gone through a bad breakup, so the wound was fresh."

With a determined look that reminded him of the old Josie, she straightened, looking ready for battle.

"All right," she said. "I'll do it. I'll go to church on Sunday. It would make Abigail happy because she keeps saying how worried she is about me that I'm not attending. If we're going to get the community involved in saving the stables, then I need to meet them where they are at."

Then she let out a broken sigh, like the

weight of the world was on her shoulders. After all, she didn't want the stables, and they represented a litany of bad memories for her. Doing this meant facing all the pain of her past, and for the first time, it occurred to Brady what an extraordinary effort she was making.

"Abigail does a weekly video chat with Laura," Josie continued. "She keeps asking me to join, but I told her I didn't think it would be a good idea. Now I'm reconsidering. I've confessed my pain to you, and you've been understanding. I gave up too easily on Laura, and I shouldn't have. Thank you."

She started to leave. Before Brady could respond, she paused at the doorway. "This doesn't mean things are fixed between us. It doesn't mean I've forgiven my father. And I'm not sure where I stand with the Lord. But I know that hanging on to all these old hurts is only punishing myself. My therapist used to tell me that I needed to learn to let go, and I would get mad, saying I didn't know how. Maybe this is how."

And then she was gone, leaving him to sit alone in the costume room, staring at the mess, wondering how to fix it, knowing that more than ever, what they needed was God's healing hand.

Chapter Five

Walking into church for the first time in nearly fifteen years wasn't as hard as Josie had anticipated. Myrna Smeathers, who had taught Josie in Sunday school, was one of the greeters at the door and was handing out the programs.

"Josie. So good to see you," she said, enveloping her in a rosewater-scented hug.

Funny, the older woman, who had always brought such cheer to Josie over the years, still smelled the same.

"Myrna. I'm so glad to see you as well. How is your family?"

Myrna beamed. "Jack Junior is still in the army, and he's up for a promotion. Still single, though, but I'm not losing hope. Who knows? Maybe you two will find a connection next time he's home."

Still the same old Myrna. The self-appointed town matchmaker, she'd taken responsibility for many of the happy marriages in town. Five years older than Josie, Jack Junior had never run in her circles, though many of her friends had often sighed over how handsome he was.

"We'll see," Josie said. "I'm much too busy for dating right now. Between trying to save the stables, and my own life in Denver, I am not sure I can fit a man into the equation."

A warm smile filled Myrna's face. "I heard that you were going to give it a go. Now, I'm not one for butting into other people's business, but I think it's a terrible shame you and Big Joe couldn't agree while he was still alive. If you ask me, he's needed you here for quite some time."

Josie hadn't asked, but that was the way of life in a small town. Everyone knew everyone's business, and they all had opinions about how things should be handled—part of why she'd dreaded coming to church.

"He had Brady," Josie said. "I wish he had relied more on him because Brady knows what he's doing. He's a smart man with a big heart for the stables. Honestly, if anyone saves the stables, it will be Brady."

Myrna nodded sagely. "You always were sweet on him. You know, he's still single as well."

Oh, boy. Josie had walked right into that one.

"I think there's been too much between us for me to have a future with Brady. You would have a better chance fixing me up with your son."

Before Myrna could answer, a man cleared his throat, and Josie turned. Brady.

On one hand, it was slightly embarrassing that he'd overheard her saying that. But on the other, it was good for him to know where he stood. She had confessed all kinds of embarrassing things about her feelings and broken heart to him. It wouldn't be right for him to think she was still carrying a torch. While she knew she had to build some kind of relationship with him, she could never trust him enough again to consider being romantically involved.

"I appreciate your vote of confidence," Brady said. He shifted his weight slightly. "But you know, I don't think I can do it alone. I'd been helping Joe all these years, trying my best, but obviously, it wasn't enough. The stables are in dire straits, and I should have seen it sooner."

It hadn't occurred to Josie that Brady

would feel responsible for all the things going wrong. "You know how stubborn my father was. You've pointed out several things you've wanted to change, but he wouldn't let you. I think, if we let you implement the different changes you had in mind, the stables will be better than ever."

"I agree," Myrna said. "You know who you need to talk to?"

Josie shook her head.

"Maddie." Myrna's face lit up. "She works over at the comfort care nursing home, and though I'm ashamed to say that that's where we have my mother, on account of her dementia being so bad, I'll tell you, Maddie puts on the best programs for the residents. I'm sure she would have some great ideas for this benefit I hear you're going to be putting on."

Myrna used to be one of the people always pushing Maddie and Josie to get along. And here it was, Josie's first day back at church, and she was already being told to date Brady and work with Maddie. If it wasn't for the fact that Myrna was the sweetest, most well-meaning human being on the planet, Josie would have gagged and rolled her eyes.

But instead, she smiled and said, "That's something Brady and I can talk about. I'm not sure Maddie would be willing, but it wouldn't hurt to try."

"What do you think you're doing, speaking for me?" Maddie demanded, stepping into their group.

Okay. Lesson learned. Josie just needed to keep her mouth shut. "Myrna mentioned what a great job you do putting on programs for the residents at the nursing home. She suggested we talk to you about some of the ideas for our benefit and see if you're willing to help."

"So you just assumed I wouldn't."

Brady held out his hands. "No. She didn't. She said she wasn't sure, but she was willing to try. I like Myrna's suggestion. Half the town tries to score invitations to the programs you do at the nursing home because they're so wonderful. You have a gift and would be an asset to any fundraiser we put on. But you need to stop assuming the worst of Josie. Coming back here, facing the pain of her past, is hard for her. And we need to step up and show her some grace and love instead of making her the enemy."

Tears pricked the back of her eyes at Brady's defense. Back when they were kids, Brady defended her all the time. But that seemed to stop once he took up with Maddie. It was silly of her to put so much stock in this one moment, but hearing Brady's acknowledgment of the difficulty of her situation made her think that maybe she wasn't so alone.

Myrna reached forward and gave Josie another hug. "Of course, this is all hard on you. You just lost your father, and while I know things weren't good between you, he was still your father, and there must still be a huge hole in your heart. I'm here for whatever you need. Once you come up with a plan, I'm going to invite you to the women's group to talk to them about volunteering and giving what they can to make your fundraiser a success."

When Myrna released her, Josie found a new sense of strength. She held dozens of fundraisers for the youth program she managed back home, but no one had ever so fervently given their support. And such a reassuring hug would have been considered unprofessional. But as Josie stepped into the sanctuary and took in the familiar sights of a place that hadn't changed in fifteen years, it almost felt like maybe she was coming home.

At the end of the service, Josie felt a deep sense of peace, unlike anything she had ever known. Though Pastor Cline couldn't have known her unease about attending when he'd planned the sermon, being reminded of the prodigal son and the importance of restoration had touched her heart. She hadn't wanted to come, but now she knew it had been exactly what she'd needed. Now she needed to take the steps toward reconciliation with the people she'd left behind.

After church, Josie greeted old friends and neighbors in the courtyard. Other than the fact that they welcomed her back, it was like she hadn't left at all. Everyone was so happy to see her. There was none of the uncomfortable feeling she'd had at her father's will reading. So many old friends surrounded her, and Josie's heart ached at the realization that she'd simply turned her back on all of them. After many quick hugs and exchanged phone numbers, as well as promises to get together as soon as she had time, Josie started toward the parking lot, where she saw Maddie getting into her truck.

"Maddie. Wait," Josie said. "I was sincere about wanting your help with the fundraiser. I trust Myrna and Brady's judgment that you do a great job at the nursing home. And, since your daughter has been part of the organization for so long, you know the families way better than I do. Would you be willing to give some thought to things we could do?"

Maddie stared at her for a moment. "Do you really want my help, or are you just trying to butter me up so I don't stand in the way of you getting back together with Brady?"

Back to this. Josie took a deep breath, trying to find the words to make Maddie feel more secure.

"What Brady and I had was a long time ago. I'm not here for a relationship with him. Even if I was, because I spend so much time working with youth, I know how important it is for them to have a stable family life with loving parents. I would never do anything to jeopardize the way the two of you co-parent Kayla."

Maddie glared at her. "You did a few weeks ago at the arena."

Josie took another deep breath, reminding herself of all the ways she had been trained to deal with difficult parents. This situation was harder because of her personal issues with Maddie, but at the heart was still a child who needed the very best from them all.

"My intention was not to undermine you as a parent. However, there were some very real safety issues, and my goal is to keep Kayla and the other children as safe as possible. I'm sorry if you felt I was undermining you. Now that we've had some time away from the situation, I'm happy to talk to you about how we can do better in the future."

Josie took out her phone and pulled up the folder of pictures and ideas. "I redid the show schedule because I remember how hard it was for people to change between some of the acts. We weren't in all the same specialty acts, so maybe you could take a look at it and make sure I covered all the bases."

She handed her phone to Maddie, who looked at it like it was a snake that was going to bite her.

"You really want my help?" Maddie asked.

"Yes." Josie gestured at the screen. "Feel free to scroll through the whole file. There are also some pictures of the old costumes so we can think about how to repurpose them since there isn't money for many new things."

Instead of looking like she was ready to work together on a solution, Maddie's eyes filled with tears. "Still trying to one-up me by being the better person."

"No," Josie said. "I don't think either one of us is better than the other. It's clear you love your daughter and want her to succeed. I know I had Abigail, but to have had a mom cheering me on would have been amazing. I would never want to take that from her. Can we please put our differences aside and work together for the best interests of Kayla?"

Maddie nodded slowly. "You asked me that before. And today, after what Pastor Cline said about living in peace with our brothers and sisters, I can't ignore the call to do better."

So God had been speaking to them both through the sermon. As much as Josie didn't want to admit it, she had been wrong to stay away from church for so long. She needed this precious time with the Lord.

With a quick, silent prayer that felt uncomfortable after so many years of unuse, Josie asked God for His help in bringing reconciliation to her and Maddie.

Maddie finally looked at the phone Josie handed to her. "This schedule is so much better. I didn't think you cared that I never had enough time to change between trick and dressage. A few of us thought that you got your father to do it that way just to make me look bad."

Wow. Funny how she'd been blamed all these years for something she had no control over. "You give me far too much credit for being vindictive, or for having any influence over my father. I always got in trouble for taking too long between ropes and trick.

Instead of changing the schedule, he told me to get faster."

"We all thought you had it made, with Big Joe as your father."

Josie had fought against that idea her whole life. But she'd never had the chance to set anyone straight. "I wish," she said. "He was really hard on me, pushing me to be better because I represented him."

A thoughtful look crossed Maddie's face. "As hard as it is to admit, you were the best." She scrolled to one of the pictures. "I loved this costume on you. I was so jealous that you got the best costume."

Josie looked at the picture. "Don't be. It was so itchy. I thought you had the cutest costume."

"It dug into my shoulders too much." Maddie laughed. "How funny that we both envied each other's costumes and never realized it until now."

Though it seemed like a simple comment, Josie wondered if that was the heart of why they'd always failed to get along.

Then she said, "Is that why you hate me so much?"

For a moment, Maddie looked thoughtful, like she couldn't even remember why she cherished this animosity against Josie. Their grudge had gone on so long that it was almost a bad habit more than anything else. Hopefully, they could find a way to move forward.

"You had everything," Maddie said. "And I lived in this dumpy trailer with a mom who was never home, and I didn't know my dad. I thought you had everything with Big Joe as your dad. I would have given anything to have even known who mine was."

The expression on Maddie's face softened, and for the first time, Josie recognized the pain in the other woman's heart. She would have never thought she could have this much compassion for her worst enemy, and she knew such grace could only come from God.

"And I wished I had known my mom," Josie said. "I can't believe it took so long for us to realize how alike our situations were. We could have supported each other better."

They spent a few minutes reminiscing about past incidents, and it amazed Josie to see how many times they ended up laughing at how it was all a big misunderstanding.

After Maddie shared a story about how she thought Josie had intentionally left her behind at a show, Josie shook her head.

"We let a lot of silly stuff come between us.

Instead of talking about the issues, we made assumptions that led to us being enemies, when we could have so easily been friends."

Maddie nodded. "You're right. We had a lot in common, but we were too busy hating each other to see it."

"Maybe we have an opportunity to redeem that," Josie said, gesturing at the phone. "Myrna thinks you have a talent for putting on events. What can you do for ours?"

After studying the pictures for a minute, Maddie said, "The ladies at the nursing home have a sewing circle. They're always looking for sewing projects to benefit charities. When I bring Kayla for her next lesson, I'll stop by and get one of each of the costumes, then talk to the ladies to see if they can do anything with them."

After all this time, Josie couldn't believe she and Maddie were having this conversation and looking at ways of working together. Josie's heart felt lighter than it had in years.

That was the freeing power that God gave them with forgiveness.

Then she held out her arms to Maddie. "I'm sorry I didn't give you more of a chance. Can we please start over?"

She half expected Maddie not to hug her

back, but Maddie did. "I would like that. I'm sorry I always saw the worst in you. I guess we both made our share of mistakes. And I'll admit that I don't always see clearly when it comes to my daughter or Brady."

Brady. That was the other thing between them.

"I don't know what happened to you guys, but if you still love him…"

Maddie shook her head. "I don't think I ever did. That's the messed-up thing about it all. At first, it was just funny to take something you wanted, but that changed when I had to grow up real fast and become the mother of a baby I wasn't prepared for. Brady was amazing—is amazing—and I couldn't do it without him. I guess I do get a little protective if I think that anything is going to take his focus off our daughter."

Even though it was good to have finally found some healing over their past, Josie was glad to bring the conversation back to the present, where they could solve their problems and make things better.

"I can understand that," Josie said. "And I hope I've put your mind at ease because for me, no matter what, Kayla is what's most important."

Maddie nodded. "So, am I still banned from the arena?"

Josie shrugged. "Are you going to be able to stop yelling instructions at her?"

Maddie laughed. "Okay, I guess I do get a little overenthusiastic. The others were right. It's not the first time I've gotten in trouble for being overzealous. I will try to keep my mouth shut."

"Then I'm willing to give you another chance there, too."

They hugged again, and it felt like something significant had shifted in their relationship. It seemed almost surreal. Josie would have never thought it possible to connect with Maddie on such a deep level.

Though Brady had told Josie that he needed her to help plan the fundraiser, Josie felt somewhat inadequate because she hadn't been around for so long. While many people in the community were familiar to her, she no longer knew the families the way she once had. She certainly didn't know the kids. But Maddie did.

A small shiver coursed through her as Josie wondered if all of this was happening as part of God's work in their lives.

When they released their embrace, Josie said, "Thanks for taking the time to talk to me about all this. There's no way I can save the stables on my own, but if we all work together, I believe we can do it."

"Okay," Maddie said. "Let me see what I can do."

As Maddie drove off, Josie felt a deep peace in her heart that she hadn't known in a long time. It was unbelievable to think that she could have reconciled with someone who'd tormented her for so long with such a simple conversation. But the truth was, the simple knowing of why and how they both envied each other for similar reasons made it easier to get past those hurts. So completely unexpected, and yet, Josie knew that this had to be God touching their hearts.

Long ago, she would have said exactly that. As much as she'd wanted to leave old Josie behind, she was glad to have finally rediscovered her.

Brady came jogging over. "Did I just see you hug Maddie?"

Josie nodded. "It does seem improbable, doesn't it? It's funny, I knew that it was Maddie and her mom alone together, but it never occurred to me that she and I were living very similar lives. Me, longing for a mother, and her longing for a father."

Brady nodded. "It's why I couldn't abandon her when she found out she was pregnant. I mean, I wouldn't be able to abandon my own kid anyway, but I always felt bad for Maddie, not having a supportive family the way I did. I didn't want my child to grow up without that."

Josie smiled at him. "I feel bad. We haven't talked about your family since I've been back. How are they?"

A wide grin filled his face. "Great. You would have seen my mom and dad today, but they're off visiting my brother Sean. He's married now and running a big ranch in Texas. They just had their first baby, and Mom is over the moon at having another little one to spoil."

Growing up, if Josie had any free time when she wasn't doing stuff for the stables, she was always at Brady's house. His mom had filled in the gaps where Abigail didn't quite understand how to mother a child when she was still a child herself. There were times when Josie would have loved to have been able to pick up the phone and give Brady's mom a call, but that would have been weird considering the circumstances.

Now that Josie was coming to terms with

the past, she was starting to remember all the good things she left behind. She'd focused on the negative, even used it to fuel herself during rough times, when she was desperately trying to move on with her life but felt so alone. Being in church today reminded her of that. That even in her loneliest moments growing up, she had the people here to comfort her, check in on her and ask her how her day was. When she'd left, she thought she had no other choice. And maybe she hadn't. But now, as much as she'd promised never to come back, she was grateful she had.

She just hoped that if they couldn't save the stables, everyone wouldn't hate her for her failure.

It would be a shame to come back and reconnect, only to let them all down again.

"I'm so glad to hear that your family is doing well," she finally said. Josie would have to trust in God and His plan and that no matter what happened, there had to be a good purpose behind it all.

"Me, too." Brady grinned. "Even though Sean is far away, he's going to do what he can to help. The ranch he runs sponsors several horsemanship events, so he's promised to talk to the owner and see what they can do for us. He's got a lot of good memories of this place, and he doesn't want to see it die."

Maybe that's what Josie needed to do with her memories of the stables. If her experience here at church could show her that a community of wonderful people had once surrounded her, could she also remember the good things about her experiences with the stables? Her therapist used to challenge her on the notion that everything here was all bad. She was right. Josie had already been planning on making an appointment when she got back home, but it felt good to realize that it wasn't just going to be about how broken she was once again, but about the growth she had been having.

Brady gestured at a group of people who had gathered in the parking lot. "A bunch of us go for brunch after church, and I thought you might want to join us. Some folks you probably remember, others are newcomers to the area, but they're all good people, and I think you would enjoy it."

Josie hesitated. While she couldn't deny all the positives that came with being back, it also felt overwhelming. She'd already dealt with so many difficult emotions; she wasn't sure she could handle much more today.

"Thanks, but I promised Abigail I'd spend some time with her today. I need to drive home tonight so I can work in the morning. I've been so busy with all the stable stuff that I haven't given her a lot of quality time."

He nodded slowly, but she could see the disappointed look on his face. She hated letting him down, but the whole reason she was doing this really was for her cousin. She had to remember her relationship with Abigail was her priority, so that, even if the stables failed, she still had her cousin. Josie had neglected their relationship a lot these past years, and the biggest lesson she'd learned in all of this was that she could no longer take Abigail for granted. Okay, maybe it was that she couldn't take anything for granted anymore.

The only trouble with deciding to open her heart again was that it was going to be hard not to let back in the man who was walking away looking slightly dejected. Yes, she was learning a lot about forgiveness and reconciliation, but she also needed to guard her heart so it wouldn't get broken again.

Chapter Six

Brady couldn't help glancing at the stack of invoices on the seat next to him as he drove back to the ranch. His meeting with the Hendersons had been enlightening, but the trouble was, he didn't know how to share the news with Josie or how to move forward. He'd hoped that understanding the billing would find them some money they didn't think they had, which was technically what happened, but it was more complicated than that.

Actually, everything was complicated. Especially when it came to his relationship with Josie. When he pulled into his spot at the stables, Josie and Kayla were standing in a group of children, lining them up to get measured for the costumes Maddie was making. Correction, Maddie was having the seniors at her senior center make. He wouldn't have believed it had he not seen it for himself, but Josie and Maddie had been getting along like old friends since their talk a month ago at church. As if to prove his point, Maddie turned to say something to Josie, and she laughed. Even better was the way Kayla had joined in. Over the last couple of weeks, Kayla had warmed to Josie, and now they were working together like it's what they'd always done.

Though Josie wouldn't want to admit it, Brady laid the credit right at the feet of God. He was getting into her heart, even if she wasn't ready to acknowledge it. Sometimes, that woman could be as stubborn as her father. And the thing was, it was one of the things he liked about her.

Which was where everything got so complicated. How could he not like her? Seeing the growth in her since she'd been back made him long for more. Yet he couldn't see how that would happen.

When he started walking toward them, a couple of the kids noticed him and ran his way. "Brady. Guess what? We're getting sparkle costumes to ride in."

Brady grinned as little Shannon Guthrie wrapped her arms around his legs in a big hug.

"I can't wait to see them!" After their hug, he picked her up and swung her around. Soon, she'd be too big for the action, but for now, it brought joy to his heart.

As she always did, Shannon swiped the hat off his head and put it on hers, giggling as she ran off. He put on his best fake mad look as he called out, "Don't make me come get you."

Shannon just laughed harder as she rejoined the line.

"Your turn to get measured," Josie said, taking the hat off the girl's head and tossing it in Brady's direction. "You should know better than to steal a cowboy's hat. Didn't anyone ever tell you that if you wear a cowboy's hat, you gotta marry him?"

Wide-eyed, Shannon stared back at her. "I can't marry Brady. He's my cousin."

Brady grinned as he looked over at Josie, trying to read the expression on her face. Did she remember that he was the one who told her that originally? Her answer had been different from Shannon's. Back then, Josie had given him that teasing smile he loved so much and said, "Then I guess it's a good thing I have every intention of marrying you."

He supposed that maybe that old wives' tale wasn't so true after all. But as he set his hat back on his head, he wished he could retreat to the days when they'd been those carefree kids who truly believed that they could conquer the world together. He missed the old Josie. The one who would tell him that with Jesus, they could do anything. The person she'd been before he broke her heart. Yes, he could admit it now. He'd done this to her. And while it was true that his daughter was the best thing in his life, he hated what it had cost him.

Josie said something to Maddie, then walked over to him. "I see you still have all the girls following you around," she said. "Do you think you can pull yourself away from your admirers long enough to see the concept we have for arranging the silent auction in the entry to the arena?"

Many of the local businesses they'd approached about donations couldn't give money, but they'd offered their goods and services, so Abigail had suggested they do a silent auction. At the rate donations were piling in, Brady was confident they'd reach their fundraising goal.

"Absolutely," he said as they walked into the arena. "That was my cousin Walt's girl, by the way," he said. "We've always had a special bond."

He didn't know why he'd felt the need to clarify his relationship to Shannon. Josie had only been joking about his admirers, and it wasn't like a nine-year-old would be a threat.

But as he remembered the girl who'd promised to marry him, and the strong, capable woman walking beside him, he'd admit to having many feelings of what if.

"I didn't know that," Josie said. "Her mother is the one who usually drops her off and picks her up."

She smiled softly, and butterflies filled Brady's stomach. Amazing how her smile could still twist him in knots. More so now that he was seeing the depth of her heart in her desire to save the stables.

"Imagine that," Josie said. "Walt all grown up with a little girl of his own. I wonder if he still thinks girls are stinky."

Brady gave a belly laugh that shook him to his toes. It had been a long time since anyone had mentioned how Walt used to say how much he hated girls. When they were kids, he'd refused to let Josie go riding with them because he said girls stank. So Josie had challenged him to a small horse race. If she won, she got to come. If he won, she'd stay home. She had beaten him soundly, and Walt was so sore over the incident, he'd refused to ride with them at all.

"I think he kind of thinks they are okay," Brady said. "He and Lindsey have three of them. It's a shame you haven't seen him with Lindsey because anyone can see just how much he adores her."

He didn't know the expression that crossed her face, but if he had to guess, it was one of regret. He hadn't thought the happy memories of the past would make her sad. Rather, he'd hoped they would remind her of more good times that would give her more reasons to stay.

Yes, he'd admit it. He wanted her to stay. Not just these visits she could squeeze in on the weekends when she was off work.

When Josie was here, things felt right.

"I've missed out on a lot," she said. "I still feel like I'm missing things by dividing my time."

She gestured at a display set up in the foyer. "Obviously, it'll be bigger and line all the walls, but this will give you an idea of what we were thinking."

"Do not let my mother make any more of those paper flowers," Kayla said, joining them. "We're running out of space in the house to store them. I'm going to have to give up my bed soon."

His heart swelled as he saw the affectionate look pass between Josie and Kayla as Josie ruffled Kayla's hair. "I like them, so if they start filling your room, you can send them to mine."

Josie picked up one of the paper flowers and held it up to her nose, even though it probably didn't smell like anything. "This just feels like happiness to me."

Probably because it was, but he couldn't say that. He'd seen the change in Josie since she'd been back, and she definitely seemed happier.

Was there a chance they could build something for the future?

The woman he couldn't get off of his mind was getting along well with his daughter and his ex. That had to count for something, didn't it?

Still, they had more pressing matters to deal with.

So, as Josie often did, he brought the subject back to the stables. "I have good news and bad news about the hay prices."

Josie tossed another flower at Kayla. "Tell your mom this one is my favorite." Kayla skipped off, and Josie turned her attention to him. "Which is?"

"The bill is correct. Your father wasn't being overcharged. A couple of years ago, the local horse rescue ran into some financial difficulties, and they didn't have enough money to pay for hay. Your father found out, and he's been paying their bill ever since. No one knew about it, because your father wanted to do his good deeds in secret."

Josie stared at him. "That doesn't sound like him. He liked to scream from the rooftops about how wonderful he was."

Brady nodded slowly. "That was the old him. In recent years, he changed. It was strange because he never talked to anyone about it. But I'd catch him doing things, like throwing a hundred-dollar bill into the bell ringer kettle at Christmas. And then there are all the people who stopped paying their fees here at the stables."

He picked up one of the brochures on the table and glanced at it. He and Josie had worked together to create it, and it felt good to see the way things were coming together.

"Yes." Josie looked thoughtful. "I confirmed with Abigail that they are all families who have hit on hard times."

He'd suspected that when he'd seen the list of people whose accounts were in arrears. "I just wish he'd talked to me about this. I could have helped him figure out how to do something with his new spirit of generosity without putting the stables in jeopardy."

"Ha!" Josie snorted. "He might have changed, but not that much."

She let out a long sigh. "And that's the trouble. How do I tell all these people he helped that we can't help them anymore? I'm afraid that when I talk to them, I'm going to have to hear about how much I let my father down."

Brady reached forward and touched her arm, letting his hand rest there for a moment. In the old days, he'd have hugged her close and given her the reassurance she was asking for. But this would have to do. "I don't think they think that at all. Everyone in town has been commenting about how pleased they are that you're stepping up to save the stables. It means a lot to everyone, and I'm sure, if your father were here, it would have meant a lot to him."

"Maybe." She kicked at the ground. "Funny how quickly I revert to being that scared little girl."

He gave her arm a final squeeze. "I know it's not the same, but I'm here for you."

The warm smile he got in return gave him hope. "Thank you. Things may have changed between us, but it does feel good to know I'm not alone."

After being back for a while, it was becoming harder and harder to remember all the reasons why Josie refused to come home. Yes, things had been hard. But there had been moments of joy as well, and as Josie saw the community coming together for the fundraiser, it was more difficult to justify staying away.

As much as she hated to admit it, the stables needed her more. The rec department had a capable staff who handled everything. Here at the stables, it was just her and Brady, along with a few dedicated volunteers, and they were all needed. She'd created such a tightly running ship at the rec center that they didn't need her as much. Sure, her coworkers did send her messages about missing her, but in reality, not a single ball had been dropped, and it was as if she wasn't gone at all.

But that was the other sad reality. The stables couldn't afford to pay Josie, and she needed money to live, which meant the job was necessary. As it was, she didn't know how much longer they could keep paying Brady. He said it didn't matter, and he was looking for another job, just in case, but if they didn't have Brady on staff full-time, there was no real way to run the stables. They were stretched thin enough with volunteer hours, and as much as Josie hated to admit it, if this fundraiser wasn't a success, she would have no choice but to sell.

Which was why, even though she hated herself for it, she agreed to meet with the developer, at least to see what kind of money was being offered and if there was a way to find a compromise that would allow them to keep at least part of the stables going.

As the shiny black SUV with a fancy corporate logo pulled into the stables lot, Josie took a deep breath and, hoping it was the right thing, said a quick prayer.

God, I know we aren't fully back together yet. But I know it seems almost humanly impossible to keep the stables going. We have more money going out than in, and these outflows benefit so many. I don't know what else to do. Help me find clarity in this meeting, and help us find a solution.

It wasn't the most eloquent prayer, but it came from the very depths of Josie's heart.

As she walked over to greet the slick man in shiny cowboy boots who had probably never seen the inside of an arena, her stomach hurt. This couldn't possibly be the answer. But she had to pursue all paths. Though she couldn't quite commit herself to say she was a Christian again, she was starting to re-embrace some of the things that she had once believed. Like the fact that God worked in mysterious ways, which meant not counting out any possibility, even the one she thought least likely.

After all, if someone had told her several months ago that she would be back at the stables, trying to save them, she would have laughed in their face.

"Good afternoon, Mr. Islington," she said, greeting the man warmly.

He gave her an equally warm smile. "Please. Call me Dean. And I must say, you are the very image of your late mother."

Josie froze. No one spoke of her mother. Not back when she was here before, not ever. Growing up, if she'd ask about her, her father would just say that she was dead and there was no sense in dwelling in the past. So it was strange to have someone almost immediately make mention of her.

"You knew my mother?"

Dean looked puzzled for a moment, then he said, "Isn't that why you called me? I'm her brother, your uncle. Your father had been talking to me about making amends, so I thought that's why you called. I thought you finally wanted to know your family."

Now it was Josie's turn to be puzzled. "I—I… There was a file on his desk from your company with a proposal to buy the stables."

Other than her father and cousins, Josie hadn't known she had any other family.

She'd learned very early on never to talk about her mother because it made her father angry. Looking back, she could see that it was his grief over losing her, but at the time, it had been confusing and painful. When she'd had to do a family tree report for school, her father had ripped the paper up and told her, "You don't need to be poking your nose into all this nonsense. We're the only family you need."

Maybe he'd thought so, but having an uncle she hadn't expected felt…

Taking a deep breath, Josie pushed the emotion aside. She had a job to do, and that was finding a way to save the stables. There'd be enough time later to deal with this unexpected family connection.

The file with the proposal had looked incomplete, so she wasn't sure how far the discussion on the sale had gone. Meeting with Dean would hopefully clarify what her father's intentions had been.

"Yes. He had approached me with an idea to buy him out. The paperwork was all but signed. We'd taken significant steps toward that end."

"I don't understand. That sounds very much unlike my father. But based on the things I've found out since taking over the stables, it seems like he changed a lot. Did he tell you why?"

Dean shrugged. "He's always kept his own counsel. But when a man gets to be a certain age, he looks at his life and his regrets, and I imagine Big Joe had more than his share. He was a hard man. There's no sugarcoating that, although I know people tend to do so once a person is gone. But he was who he was, and it caused a lot of pain."

Even though Josie had been working very hard at trying to forgive her father, it felt good to have someone acknowledge that her father wasn't the wonderful man everyone here wanted to make him out to be. She'd always figured her father's pain at her mother's death was so great that he clammed up about her. But to keep Josie from knowing her mom's family seemed about more than his grief.

"I'm trying to work through that," she said. "But it seems like the longer I'm back, the more confused I am about everything."

The understanding look Dean gave her brought reassurance to her troubled heart. "When he first called, I was angry, too. He'd taken Kathleen away from us, and then she died, and he wanted nothing to do with us."

"I didn't even know you existed," she said.

"Kathleen met him at one of those shows you people put on. She was enamored of this smooth-talking cowboy from a world completely different from our own. Islington Holdings is one of the largest real-estate-development companies in America. Headquartered in Chicago. Her world was completely about the city, and she knew nothing of the kind of life your father offered, and it intrigued her. But it was harder than she imagined, and she struggled with this way of life. When she died, we blamed your father, even though now, we know it was no one's fault. Sometimes these things happen. But none of us were willing to let go of our grudges."

He let out a long sigh, then gestured around

the property. "When you were a little girl, we'd tried to create one of our master communities down the road. Your father was one of the driving forces in stopping us, and eventually, that land was turned into a nature preserve. It cost us millions of dollars to fight, and it would have cost even more to build, but then we backed out."

Josie remembered. Her father would rant and rave about greedy corporations trying to ruin their way of life. When they had found out that an endangered bird species used the area for their nesting, the whole community had mobilized to create the preserve. Josie and the youth group had even made protest signs and had spent a night camped out in what was to become the preserve.

Brady had told Josie that he thought it was silly to try to save a bunch of birds, but he'd helped her anyway.

Kind of like now. It seemed silly to do all this work to save the stables, but they were important to the community, and even though it seemed hopeless to try, just like in creating the nature preserve, who knew how God could work things out in the situation?

Maybe God was getting more under her skin than she'd admitted to everyone else.

"So why would my father contact you about buying the stables for you to develop the land?"

Dean smiled. "I think it was his way of apologizing for everything that happened between us. He kept us from you. And he ruined a lot of business for us here, and this was the closest to an apology he could give."

It sounded a lot like what her father would do. Far be it for him to say he was sorry if he was too hard on her, but he would do things like buy her a new piece of tack or the equivalent and think it made up for everything.

"So why did he give me the stables? How is that an apology?"

Dean gestured around the grounds. "This place has been losing money for years. I'm surprised you're even attempting to save it. You won't be able to raise the money. I don't think he ever intended for you to save it. I think he wanted you to sell it to me, giving you all the money. From what I understand, he cut you off without a cent. It must have been hard for you, going it alone at first."

Josie had thought of it that way, but it still didn't feel right, letting the community suffer. And it still didn't explain her father's bigheartedness in so many different ways, especially since so much of his secret generosity had been focused on helping various members of the community.

"I don't know what you're looking for, so why don't I show you around? You can tell me about your plans, and we'll see if we can come to an agreement."

As they walked the grounds, Dean spent more time talking to her about his family and the past, as well as about his plans to develop the area. It was strange to hear so much about her mother. In just one short hour, she learned more about her than she'd heard her entire life. But by the end of the tour, Josie didn't have peace about selling to Dean, family or not. When Josie showed him important parts of the stables, including more historical aspects, Dean seemed completely uninterested in them.

They paused at one of the old outbuildings, originally an important stage stop along the Santa Fe Trail. Down the road was a history museum outlining the important contribution their community had made to this historic trading route.

"This here is an example of the history I was telling you about," she said. "I know it doesn't look like much, but my father always dreamed of doing something to preserve it."

Dean frowned. "Is this on the exact route?"

Josie shrugged. "I don't know. I'm sure my father had the documentation somewhere in his mess. I just know this was always a source of pride for him, being part of such an important part of history."

"Well, I hope not. Or at least that one of those history maniacs doesn't cause any problems. The rest of the investment team was nervous about pursuing this project because of the trouble we had last time. But you're a sensible girl, which means that you understand the value of the land is much more important than its past."

Oh, boy. That wasn't what she meant by any of this at all. History was important to her, and she wanted to do what she could to preserve it.

"But what if it is of historical significance?"

Dean stared at her. "I wouldn't say anything if I were you."

He paused and jammed his hands in his pockets. "Look, I think we both know that you aren't going to save the stables. The only thing of value here in this place is the land. I'm going to bulldoze everything and build one of the master communities our group is known for. Based on the land values in the area and what we can make, and the fact that you are my niece, I'm going to give you top dollar. I'm willing to do better than the agreement I gave your father. As long as you don't live too extravagant of a lifestyle, I can almost guarantee that you'll never have to work again."

It sounded almost too good to be true. But the thing was, Josie didn't come into this situation looking for money, and she didn't want it now. She might feel irrelevant at her job, but that didn't mean that she didn't see herself working in some capacity to help others. Maybe she hadn't known her father that well anymore, but she did know that for him, the value of life was all about hard work.

Just another piece of the mystery of her life, she supposed. Still, she didn't disagree with the idea that saving the stables would be an uphill battle.

Josie smiled at him again as they arrived back at Dean's SUV. "Thank you so much for coming out today. I'll let you know about your proposal, and I hope we can stay in touch. Maybe sometime we could get together, and I could learn more about my family."

Dean held his arms out to her. "I'd like that. Any chance I could get a hug from my niece?"

"Of course." Josie hugged him tight, and since she had never gotten a hug from her mother, having one from someone so connected to her was like finding a new link to her mom. She resolved to stay in touch with this man, to learn more about her mother's family and, if possible, to find forgiveness in her heart for her father keeping her away from them.

When he released her, he said, "Think about my offer. You have a life in Denver, and from what I've seen, it's a good one. Don't be like your mother and throw it all away on these stables. It might have been no one's fault, but like her, this isn't where you were meant to be."

He gestured at her outfit. While she had chosen to be a little more practical than the skirt and heels that she had chosen for her return visit, and she was finally back in normal shoes, she also wasn't going back to the old Josie, who wasn't allowed to wear the pretty, fashionable clothing that she enjoyed. Today she wore boots, but they were pretty ones, and she wore jeans with just a little bling and a feminine flowered top that didn't completely belong in the stables, but made her feel like herself. Was there a way to be both city girl and country girl? She didn't know, but she was going to give it her best try.

However, it didn't seem right to contradict this man, who saw that she was so much like the sister he desperately missed. She couldn't fault him for that. And the truth was, while she disagreed with his assessment, she was also still learning about who she was. She might have agreed with him a couple of months ago.

As he pulled out of the drive, Brady approached. "Who was that?"

"The investor I was talking about."

A dark expression crossed his face. "From the way you hugged him, it looks like it was a good conversation. I thought you weren't going to entertain the idea of selling until after we saw what the benefit did."

Josie took a deep breath. She had known that even talking to any potential investors would be difficult, but it was important to keep her options open.

"I have to look at all possibilities. It doesn't mean I'm going to sell."

The expression on his face didn't change. "That looked a lot friendlier than a simple business deal."

"So, my father didn't tell you about this investor?"

Brady shook his head. "Why would he?"

"Point taken. But once you understand who he is and why my father contacted him, I think you'll see things a little differently."

She went on to explain everything Dean had told her. He shared the same amazement and disbelief she'd had, which only made sense because he'd seen the loneliness of her childhood and the desire for a connection to her mother.

"That's something," he said when she finally finished her story. "I guess this makes it easier for you to decide to sell, given that it would put you back in touch with your mother's family."

Josie shook her head. "No. I made a promise to you and Abigail." Then she gestured around the property. "And to our community. As I was showing him around, the thing I realized is what a rich history we do have. My uncle didn't seem to care about that, and why would he? They're all in Chicago and have no connection to this. Honestly, even if I did sell, it wouldn't feel right selling to someone who didn't care about the community. I think I would try to find a buyer who wanted to invest in this place and wanted to see our community thrive."

"Did you tell him that?"

Josie shook her head. "I didn't. I hadn't thought of it that way until I spoke to you, but now that I have, it feels like the right thing."

"I know it's a lot for you to take in," he said. "But please understand that, unlike you, the rest of us don't have a backup plan."

She could see where this would make him nervous, and at least she had the way to reassure him. "I would never leave any of you hanging. If I do sell, I can promise you that most of the money is going to the people who have invested their lives in this place. My uncle said something about thinking that maybe my father did this to ensure I would be taken care of, but that's never been my goal. I don't need money. Sure, money is nice, but I've always been happy with what I have. My life is good. So I would use the money from the sale to help all of you."

"I didn't ask for a handout," Brady said, glaring at her. "This has never been about the money for me, either. I've got enough time and experience in the volunteer fire department here, and I've helped with enough wildfires and things like that that I'm known among firefighters. If all I wanted was a job to help people, I could easily apply to any fire department in the area and be hired. Probably better pay, too, than what the stables can afford. But I want to help these people here. They mean something to me, and writing a check isn't going to fix that."

Brady stormed off, leaving Josie standing there, shell-shocked. He'd never raised his voice to her, not in all the years she'd known him. It hurt in a strange new way that she hadn't expected. Back in the day, his approval and understanding had meant everything to her. Now, in the wake of the revelations about her mother's family, she needed that understanding more than ever.

As she watched him retreat into the barn, she realized that she'd been so focused on her own confusion and worry that she'd deeply hurt him without meaning to. She ached to make it right.

She could deny it all she wanted, but the truth was, she did still care about Brady. Maybe it was time for her to sort out those feelings and what they meant, and how to get a real grip on them.

Chapter Seven

Brady couldn't remember being so angry in his entire life. He knew Josie was just being honest. And speaking from a place that didn't include having faith. Oh, he was certain she thought she was looking out for his best interests, but he had a hard time realizing how little she really did know of him.

He strode into the barn, hoping to take refuge in his office, even though he wasn't sure what that would solve. But at least it got him away from Josie.

They were supposed to be in this together, and she'd gone ahead and met with some investor. Showed what kind of faith she had. Which was none, and he knew that. But he'd also hoped that maybe she had learned something from all of this.

Something deep down bothered him even more, and as he figured that out, sadness replaced his anger. If Josie sold the stables, he'd be unlikely to see her again. She'd have no need to visit the community he still called home.

This wasn't just a job to him. He had other options. And not just as a firefighter. His brother could have gotten him a job on a neighboring ranch. But he wanted to give this experience to his daughter.

He hadn't wanted to upend her life or even try to figure out what a change like that would be for Maddie.

And speaking of, she was standing at the edge of the arena, looking peeved about something. Though their relationship had significantly improved since Maddie and Josie had made up, Brady still didn't want to deal with Maddie in a bad mood. If it was about Kayla, Maddie would call or text.

As he passed the conference room, he saw the boxes of invitations sitting on the table. He and Josie were supposed to be working on them together, but he needed to do something productive for the sake of the benefit. Maybe Josie had her doubts, but he was going to give it his all.

He opened the boxes and began laying out the invitations and envelopes. Originally, they weren't going to be so fancy, but one of the parents owned a print shop, and she'd volunteered to donate nice invitations for their VIP guests, in addition to the flyers that were plastered all over town.

How could Josie think they wouldn't succeed when they had so much community support?

"You're not going to get very far without these," Josie said, standing in the doorway, holding up a set of pens and the mailing list. "I know you're frustrated with me, but I hope you know that I'm not giving up, either."

The sweet smile on her face took his breath away. He was supposed to be mad at her, and yet this one simple gesture made the bad feelings brewing inside him completely dissipate.

"I don't know what to think," he said. Though he wanted to stay mad at her, he could see that this was her version of a peace offering. Which he'd take, since it was an effort to save the stables.

When she entered the room, she had a hand behind her back. "I also thought we could use some good working snacks."

Then she tossed a giant package of gummy

bears onto the table. "It's been a while, but this used to be our favorite study snack. I saw you stealing some of Kayla's the other day, so I'm pretty sure you still like them."

The simple gesture brought a smile to his face. Not just in the memory of their past, but the fact that she'd taken the time to notice his present.

He smiled and patted the chair next to him. "I guess we'd better get to work then."

Josie took the seat indicated and immediately opened the bag.

"Hey," he said. "I thought those were for me."

Josie grinned. "I said *we* could use a snack. I got the big bag on purpose."

He loved that smile on her. More than that, he loved her thoughtfulness in setting this up. But it didn't fix things between them.

"I'm still upset with you," he said. "It feels like you're giving up too soon."

Josie gestured at the items on the table in front of them. "Does this look like I'm giving up? I'm sitting beside you, working toward the same goal. What you fail to understand is that we need to look at all options, even the ones we don't like. You say we need to put our faith in God, but you've also said that

God doesn't always work in the way we want Him to. If that's true, then shouldn't we pursue all avenues, not just the ones we want?"

He hadn't thought of it that way, and as much as he hated to admit it, Josie was right. He'd been saying he wanted God's will, but if he was being honest, he had only considered solutions that involved keeping the stables open.

Josie looked at him intently, then said, "I know it seems like, at times, your words to me about prayer and God have been falling on deaf ears. But I have been listening, and I have been seeking Him in prayer. Surely you can see that if I wanted the easy way out, I would have taken it from the very beginning."

She reached over and squeezed his hand. "I know things between us have changed, and we can't go back to what we once had. But I'd like to think that we've come to a place where we can trust each other again, even if it's just a little bit."

His throat tightened, and the sensation of her hand in his brought him to a deeper place of humility than he could remember having ever been in. He'd been so focused on who she used to be, and the changes in her, that he'd failed to recognize the incredible woman she had become.

"I do see that," he said. "I'm sorry I haven't given you enough credit. I'll do better. And I'm also sorry I wasn't more understanding about your meeting your uncle for the first time. That must have been a terrible shock."

She nodded and looked down, clearly overcome with emotion. "A shock, but I wouldn't call it terrible. I now have a connection to my mother, and I intend to pursue it."

After swallowing the lump in his throat, he continued, "If you don't mind, I'd like to pray for us."

Josie smiled, and for the first time, instead of seeing her lack of faith, he saw instead a renewed depth and genuine desire to do what was pleasing in the Lord's sight. Clearly there were still things he could learn about faith from her.

As he prayed, for the first time, he gave over his insistence on saving the stables, and prayed that whatever happened to the stables be used to glorify the Lord. He'd seen the stables as his only way, but that just showed he was relying on himself, not the Lord.

It was the most freeing prayer he'd offered

in he didn't know how long. When he was done, Josie had tears in her eyes.

"That was beautiful," she said. "Would it be okay if I hugged you?"

He nodded as he held his arms out to her, and she fell into them like it was the most natural place for her to be. Like she'd never left.

When she pulled away, he immediately missed her warmth. He still didn't know what was going to happen with their relationship, but he lacked the previous anxiety he'd had over it. Suddenly he didn't need to have the answers. He didn't need to go back to where they'd once been. But he sure hoped that they could find something new.

He'd be lying if he said he didn't want to see where it could go romantically, but he would also accept if it didn't go in that direction.

Josie handed him one of the pages from the stack of papers she brought in. "Okay, we need to get to work. You start with this list."

Then she reached into the bag of gummy bears and tossed one at him. "And now you have sustenance."

Her smile made him want to take her back into his arms. But she was right. They had work to do. Now that he had given over this task to God, he felt less pressure, and more lighthearted.

He'd gotten two of the invitations filled out and addressed when Kayla walked in.

"Oh, please tell me you're not letting Dad do that," she said.

Brady looked down at his handiwork. "What? It needs to get done."

Kayla gestured at the invitations he'd painstakingly addressed. "Your handwriting is terrible."

Patting the empty seat on the other side of her, Josie said, "If you think you can do better, join us. As your father said, it has to get done."

The look on Kayla's face was priceless. She could criticize all she wanted, but then she had to be willing to do the work.

"We have gummy bears," Josie said.

Kayla grinned and reached for the bag. "Wow, you got the big one. Mom and Dad never get the big one."

Josie grabbed the bag. "Gummy bears are only for worker bears."

"Fine," Kayla said, plopping down into the seat. "Give me a list and some invitations. Dad says we all have to do our part, so I'll do it. Plus, I can practice my calligraphy."

Josie tossed a handful of gummy bears at Kayla, then set the bag back down in the middle of the table. The look of affection that passed between them warmed his heart. This was what Brady had always wanted for him and his daughter. For him to be able to bring a woman into his life that he could care for, but who also cared for Kayla.

Was the key to having his prayers answered as simple as relinquishing his will to allowing God's to prevail? Not that it was about coming up with a formula, because he knew better than to think that way. But it was interesting how such clarity of vision came with a simple relinquishing of his will over to God.

They got to work addressing the envelopes, and at times, it was hard to stay focused on the task at hand, because he would look over at Josie and see her connection with his daughter, and it just felt so right. Like this was how things were meant to be.

"There you are," Maddie said, entering the conference room. "We need to get home so you can help me get the supplies ready for the Sunday school lesson I'm teaching tomorrow."

Kayla looked up from the invitation she was working on. "Can Dad bring me home later? I'm having a lot of fun working on the invitations. I'm using what I learned from that calligraphy set you got me for Christmas."

Maddie looked slightly put out by Kayla's answer. Though things were improving in their relationship, it was clear that didn't mean she liked having her plans for Kayla thwarted. Even though they were sharing a precious moment, Brady recognized that the joy in this was also about letting Maddie have similar time with Kayla. This, too, was another thing that felt right to give to the Lord. The gratitude for the blessing he had in this moment, but also the ability to let it go because he had confidence that there would be more.

"Your mom needs you," Brady said. "You've been a big help here, so don't let your mom down."

Kayla glanced longingly at the bag of gummy bears. "Can I take some for the road?"

Josie's laugh warmed his heart. "As long as it's okay with your mom," she said. "I don't want to ruin her plans for your supper."

Kayla looked at her mom with the puppy-dog eyes Brady had always struggled to resist.

"Please, Mom? Josie even got the big bag,

so they won't miss any. You never get the big bag."

A dark look crossed Maddie's face. They might have found a way to get along, but that didn't mean Maddie wasn't still extremely overprotective of her relationship with her daughter. That was something they were going to have to figure out.

Josie seemed to sense that, and she said, "I only got the big bag so that we had plenty to share in the work session. I didn't know how many would be coming to help us, but if I'd intended to get you gummy bears, it would have been a much smaller bag."

Some of the tension slid off Maddie's face. Yes, she was jealous. One of the reasons why Brady had found it so hard to date was that he'd never been able to get Maddie to understand that he was never going to allow a woman he brought into his life be a substitute for her as a mother. Despite all their disagreements over the years, the one thing he could not deny was that Maddie was a good mother who loved their daughter very much.

"I suppose a couple won't hurt," Maddie said. "Even though I'm sure you have probably eaten more than your fair share."

Josie laughed. "I would say that's a toss-up between the two of them. Like father, like daughter, I guess. She might have inherited your skill for trick riding, but she's definitely got her father's sweet tooth."

Laughing along with her, Brady said, "Hey now. I was a good trick rider."

Maddie laughed, another sign she was finally relaxing, and hopefully feeling more secure about the situation. "Yes, but you spent way more time in the dirt than any of us combined."

It felt good to hear Josie laughing with her, even if it was at his expense. They were not wrong, but he also wasn't going to let them get the last word in.

"I learned a lot from falling. That's the thing about mistakes. It's not a failure if you've learned something from it."

Funny how what he'd meant as a light-hearted response to their joking was wisdom he'd needed to hear himself. Yes, he'd made a lot of mistakes, but he was still here, learning and growing. And that was the hope for them all. He smiled as he looked at the three women in the room and said a prayer of gratitude for the blessings they had brought into his life.

Kayla grabbed a handful of gummies and

tossed a couple into her mouth, then leaned over and gave Josie a hug. "Thanks for sharing your gummy bears and letting me help. This was more fun than I thought it would be."

Once again, Brady's heart warmed at the sight of the affection between the person he loved most in the entire world and a woman he was coming to care for very deeply.

Kayla turned and hugged him. "'Bye, Dad. Love you."

He kissed her on top of the head, contentment filling him.

"Love you, too," he said.

She popped another gummy bear in her mouth. "Save me some of these. You'll get a stomachache if you eat them all."

Brady laughed. "Gummy bears are for workers only."

Kayla grabbed one of the empty boxes, then tossed some invitations and the list she'd been working from into it. "Fine. I'll do more tonight when I'm watching my show."

She looked thoughtful for a moment, then grabbed one of the legal pads sitting on the table that she'd used to practice some of her strokes on. "Is it okay if I take this as well? I like the feel of the paper for practicing better than the calligraphy paper I have at home. It's a different texture."

Josie glanced at the pad. "Sure. My father had probably dozens of them lying around. If you like that paper so much, remind me next time you're here, and I'll give you some of the ones I don't think we have any use for."

He would have never guessed that the offer of some old legal pads would make his daughter so happy. But again, this simple exchange only served to give him more hope that there was a chance things could work out between them all.

"Thank you," Kayla said, returning to Josie and giving her another hug. "I didn't think I would like that calligraphy set my mom got me for Christmas so much, but the more I play around with it and the different pens and papers, I'm starting to think it was the best gift ever."

He glanced at Maddie to see her soft smile, and that feeling of hope increased. Yes, they were figuring this out.

Josie closed the lid of her laptop and rubbed her eyes. She'd liked to have said that they were making incredible progress on the show, which they were, but it seemed like it just wasn't enough.

But they still had two months before the show, which meant there was still hope. She glanced at the clock. Though they usually didn't practice on Sundays, the trick riders had asked for the extra practices after church to make sure they had their tricks solid for the show. Kayla had asked her to come watch her trick today, and it felt good to see how the teenager was starting to trust her. Not that Josie and Brady were even close to coming to that point, but sometimes Josie found herself wondering what if. She had too much on her plate, though, to give it any serious consideration. Between her full-time job, trying to save the stables, mending her relationship with her cousins and getting to know her newfound uncle, she was over capacity to deal with these new growing emotions.

She walked past Brady's office, where Brady looked like he was studying a spreadsheet.

"You're going to miss Kayla ride," she said, leaning in the doorway.

Brady grabbed his hat off his desk and set it on his head. "Yeah, I know. I was just hoping to get a little further on figuring out these numbers. The Garcias have been great about showing me the information I need to come up with to create a good working budget for the stables, but your father didn't keep it in an organized way that anyone else could understand."

Josie laughed as he stepped out into the corridor with her. "And yet he could find everything so easily. It's really frustrating trying to figure out his system. I'm so glad the Garcias were willing to donate their time to help you sort through it."

They walked outside toward the main arena. "That's what gives me the most hope for the stables," Brady said. "We aren't where we need to be, but I'm finding that the more I get word out, the more people come from unexpected places willing to help."

When they got to the arena, Kayla was already warming up. Maddie was sitting by herself in the stands, looking like she was studying some papers.

Josie started toward her, but Maddie held up a folder. "I'm trying to get some work done in between when Kayla rides," Maddie said.

Even though Maddie was slightly curt, it was nice that Maddie felt comfortable enough to tell her when it wasn't a good time to sit together.

"No problem," Josie said. "I peeked in on the costume room last night, and the costumes are looking great. I'll leave you to your work, but I didn't want to let an opportunity to tell you how impressed I am pass us by."

Maddie looked up at her and smiled. "Thank you. The residents at the nursing home have been working really hard. It's been great to see their enthusiasm. I just hope it's not all for nothing."

The tension in her voice was obvious, and it occurred to Josie that a lot of people had their hopes riding on the success of the stables' fundraiser. Their community was coming together in a powerful way, and even though Josie and Brady had brought themselves to an acceptance of God's will, regardless of the outcome, not everyone had had that same epiphany. Josie wasn't sure how she would handle their disappointment if they failed.

Brady joined Josie at the base of the stands, standing close enough she could feel his warmth, and it comforted her. They were becoming a team in a way they had never been before—stronger, better—and though she still had her moments of longing for the past, what they were achieving now seemed more than anything she could have imagined.

"We're doing everything we can," Brady said to Maddie. "You've been a big part of that, and I hope you know just how much it means to me."

Instead of accepting his praise, Maddie looked a bit grumpy. "The stables have been a huge part of my life, as well as our daughter's. Of course I'm going to do everything I can to help."

She looked like she was going to say something else, then she gestured at the arena. "Kayla is about to go."

Josie turned and watched as Kayla performed the full stroud, one of the tricks she had been struggling with when Josie first got here, flawlessly.

"Woo!" Brady yelled, his excitement contagious as the stands thundered with applause. He looked at Josie, his eyes shining. "Did you see that?"

Then he turned back to look at Maddie. "Wasn't that amazing? Our little girl."

As Kayla rode back to her place in line, and her instructor began talking to her, the grin on her face told Josie that she was also pleased with her performance.

Even Maddie looked happy, and once again, Josie felt hopeful for the future. Though she also reminded herself again that even though there had been small moments of affection and what-ifs, Josie and Brady had not even come close to discussing what things might look like between them as a couple.

Brady gestured at a different spot in the bleachers. "I guess we'd better let Maddie get back to her work, so we can sit over here and watch."

Brady sat next to her, closer than usual, and his nearness brought butterflies to her stomach. She could get used to this. She would have never imagined herself sitting back here at the stables and feeling such contentment. But as she looked across the grounds, where another group of children were working in another arena, and horses were playing in the paddock in the distance, she felt like, dare she say it, this was where she belonged.

One of the moms approached Josie. "I heard you were looking for volunteers for grounds cleanup. I couldn't help but notice how some of the landscaping is looking a bit worn. Our family owns a landscaping company, and if you'd be willing to feature us in the program, as well as get some volunteers to help with the labor, I'd be happy to help with a refresh. I hope you don't mind, but I took the liberty of making some drawings."

The woman handed her some pages, and they were absolutely perfect. Far better than anything Josie could have come up with on her own.

"You would donate this to us?" she asked.

Brady looked over at the drawings as well. "Grace, this is amazing. I've always wanted to do more with the landscaping here, to make it look nicer, but I could only do so much."

Brady's energy was contagious, and it sent chills up and down her spine.

"I just want to make sure we put our best foot forward for the fundraiser," Grace said. "When people come here for the show, I want them to love this place as much as we do. But right now, it's a little rough around the edges."

Josie didn't disagree, and from the thoughtful murmur from Brady, she knew he felt the same way. In moments like these, it felt like they couldn't possibly fail.

"I accept," Josie said. "Kayla is about to go again, so is there any way you could stop by the office after this ride so we can go over details and you can let me know what we need to provide?"

"Of course," Grace said. "Kayla and the rest of the girls are looking wonderful, and I know it's all because of the time you took to teach them those abdominal exercises a couple weeks ago. I'm so glad that you decided to give the stables another chance. It means a lot to all of us."

As Grace left, the warmth flooding Josie's heart filled her with such gratitude that Brady and Abigail had pushed her to do so many hard things and face her past.

When she looked over at Brady, he smiled at her, and once again, she couldn't help wondering if maybe they had a chance at a future together.

Chapter Eight

It had been a month since they had prayed to allow God's will to prevail in the stables, even if it meant losing them. As Brady looked at the latest balance sheet, he felt a sense of peace in knowing that they had given it all over to God. The numbers still didn't look good, but he thought they were making progress, with one month to go before the big show.

In addition to the help he was getting with the books and the landscaping, some of the parents were pitching in with costumes along with Maddie's senior sewing group, and others were seeking out sponsorships and donations for the stables. No, it didn't cover the income they needed, but it gave them the other things they did need to make the fundraiser a success.

But at this point, they still desperately needed cash.

Despite Josie's objections, he'd refused to draw a paycheck this month. He figured he had enough in savings that he could go six months without a salary if he had to.

Josie walked into his office, and he smiled.

"Are those our latest financial reports?" she asked.

It was starting to get frustrating how much he loved that smile. Sometimes he forgot how deep the divide was between them. She'd clearly just come from spending the week in Denver and, from the way she was dressed, directly from the office. Today, she wore a pretty floral dress that made her look like she was headed to a garden party instead of the stables. A lump formed in his throat as he remembered the young girl who just wanted to be pretty, and now here was this amazingly beautiful woman standing before him.

Kayla came bounding into the office. "Miss Josie. You're back."

Kayla threw her arms around Josie, and Josie gave his daughter a big hug. It wasn't just Josie's outward appearance that made her so beautiful, but it was also her incredible giving heart.

"Yes," Josie said. "I was able to get off work a little early, and I was hoping to get to see today's trick practice. Are you still doing those ab exercises that I showed you?"

Though Brady could have told Josie that he had never seen his daughter so enthusiastic about exercising, it was far more rewarding to see Josie smile at Kayla's enthusiastic nod.

"Yes. I've been getting together with some of my teammates, and we do them while bingeing on our favorite show."

Josie gave Kayla another squeeze. "That's fantastic. What a great way to multitask."

The way his daughter lit up at Josie's encouragement warmed Brady's heart. He'd always said that he wanted a woman who loved his daughter as much as he did. He thought it impossible, but watching Kayla and Josie together gave him hope. If only he could figure out how to know how to be the man Josie deserved.

His daughter chatted with Josie for a few more minutes, and it was all he could do not to stare at them both in awe and pride. He knew that Josie's job required she work well with children, but her special touch with Kayla was more than just "work." Josie simply had a gift for making people feel like they belonged.

Two girls who rode trick with Kayla, Raine and Elizabeth, entered the office. "Our costumes came in, and they're terrible. Your mom says we're stuck with them, but they're absolutely hideous."

The tragic wail from Raine rang with high teenager drama, and Brady had to hide a smile. From the look on Josie's face, she was doing the same.

"I'm sure we can salvage them," Josie said. "If not, there's a dance-supply store in Denver that I've used for some of our rec-center programs. I can talk to the owner and see if she's willing to do anything for us."

The girls squealed gleefully, but Josie held up a hand. "I just said I'd talk to her. Maddie is in charge of the costumes, so whatever I work out, we still have to get Maddie's approval."

Kayla groaned. "Which means we'll be stuck with the ugly costumes forever. If it were up to my mom, we would never have anything cute. She's no fun."

The other girls groaned along with her, then Kayla looked over at Josie. "Why can't she be fun like you?"

Josie shook her head. "Don't say things like that. She's your mom, and she's a great mom. I get to be fun because I'm not your parent, but trust me, I'm sure I would be just as 'no fun' as all of your moms if I were your parent."

Once again, Brady was impressed with how deftly Josie handled the situation. All the girls on the team were bonding with her and had developed a deep level of admiration for her. He could see now why Josie had spoken so passionately about making a difference in children's lives. She truly had a knack for this work, and if she gained the trust of the kids in the rec program as well as she had with these girls, he could see where she was a valuable asset to that program.

And just as quickly as they had had their moment, the girls started giggling about an actor they liked doing something on social media, then they ran off, pulling out their phones to watch whatever video they'd been talking about.

"Kids," Brady said, laughing. Then, as he heard more giggles down the hall, he said, "Wait. I don't think I've seen that video. I need to call them back to make sure it's appropriate."

Josie laughed. "I have seen that one more

times than I care to count. But move over, and I'll show you."

She came behind his computer and, with a few quick strokes, had the video pulled up. He should have been paying more attention to the video, but all he could think about was how good she smelled, like sunshine and hay, with something a little sweet thrown in.

Absolutely delightful.

Josie started laughing, and he realized that he'd missed most of the video. So much for trying to be a good father and monitor what his daughter was consuming on social media. But he trusted Josie, and when he finally dragged his attention to the computer screen as he should have been doing, he had to admit, this guy all the kids were laughing about was pretty funny.

"Thank you for sharing with me," he said. "Parenting seems so much harder these days than when we were young because we didn't have all of these other things to worry about. Some days I don't know if I'm sinking or swimming."

Josie gave him a warm smile as she squeezed his shoulders gently. "You're doing a wonderful job. Kayla is so blessed to have a father like you."

And just as quickly as that moment began, Josie moved away, taking her warmth and making him miss her, even though she was still standing right there.

"Now that we have a moment of peace," Josie said, "I found some of the old rosters from the early days of the stables. I was talking to Abigail and Laura, and we thought we could reach out to some of the alumni for their support."

Brady stared at her. "Laura is helping?"

Josie nodded. "Yes. After the first couple of awkward family video chats, Laura and I have been talking a lot more. I told her how much healing I have been finding as I've been working with you and Abigail, as well as the rest of the community, to save the stables. We've come to a place of forgiveness over the past, and I truly believe that we are finding a new level of unity as a family."

Her eyes got a little misty as her shoulders rose and fell like she was taking a deep breath. "I didn't think any of this was possible, and as angry as I was at my father for everything, and I thought that leaving me the stables was the worst possible thing he could have done to me, I'm now starting to realize what a gift it was. I may not have found reconciliation with him, but I have my cousins, my mother's family and this community as a result."

Then, as she always did when she got emotional, she squared her shoulders and pulled a paper out of her bag.

"Laura is tracking down our old members and creating an alumni directory. I've done a lot of grant writing for my job, so I have Abigail researching grants and the information we need to obtain them. Obviously, the grant is a longer-term strategy, but we said we'd explore all avenues, and this is one."

If that wasn't enough to make him completely fall for her, Brady wasn't sure anything else would have done the job. Josie was the whole package. Beautiful, tenderhearted, smart and willing to learn and grow. What more could he ask for?

But he'd hurt her, and he still couldn't see how he could deserve someone as wonderful as her.

"This all sounds great," Brady said. "We're a good team. I know how to handle the general operations of a stable, but what you're doing is way beyond my skill set. Together, we stand a real chance of saving the stables."

As he saw the light shining in her eyes, he

could feel the hope coming from her. God had been doing great work in them all, and he was grateful for it.

After Josie's meeting with Brady, she felt a lot more optimistic than she had about everything in a while. Just being in his presence was often enough to raise her spirits. It was almost like when they were teenagers, when no matter what mood she'd been in, Brady always made her feel a little bit better. She paused at the entrance to the sewing room, where Maddie was working on one of the costumes.

"Hey, Maddie," Josie said. "How's everything going?"

Maddie didn't turn around, so Josie came into the room and around the side of the table. It was obvious her friend had been crying.

"Is everything okay?"

Josie moved to sit next to Maddie, but Maddie waved her off. "Please. Just go. I need to deal with this on my own."

Taking a deep breath, Josie examined Maddie's face, red and puffy, and from the hard-set look to her eyes, it was clear she just wanted to be alone.

"Okay," Josie said. "But if you do feel like

talking, or if I could help in any way, please let me know. I'm here for you."

She squeezed Maddie's shoulder, but Maddie shrugged her off, so Josie left the room. She got a few feet from the door when she spied Kayla.

"Josie." Kayla's bright smile filled her face as she ran to Josie and gave her another hug. That was the rewarding thing about working with children—that they were all so free to show their affection once it had been earned.

"Did you girls finish watching your videos?"

Kayla's face lit up. "Yes. And we have the best idea for our costumes."

"Great. You should tell your mom and see what she thinks."

Instead of looking happy that Josie was supportive, Kayla's face fell. "I don't think so. She's in a really bad mood. We were hoping to tell you, and you would approve it."

Josie sighed. If Kayla had just gone in to talk to Maddie, given Maddie's upset appearance, she could see where Kayla might be hesitant to share her costume idea. Maybe Maddie had a bad day at work or something. But with Maddie, it was best not to push until she was ready.

"We're not going to go behind your mom's back," Josie said. "Number one, she is in charge of costumes. Number two, she's your mom, and I don't want you to think that you can't talk to her. Maybe now isn't the best time, but why don't you tell me what your idea is, and I'll help you prepare a presentation for her?"

The smile filling Kayla's face warmed Josie's heart. She'd had similar conversations with many children in her programs over the years, and it was always so gratifying to see how Josie's work with them ended up bringing parent and child closer together. Not that there was anything wrong with Maddie and Kayla's relationship, because aside from the usual teenage mother-daughter squabbles, they seemed to get along well.

"That would be great," Kayla said. "I really want her to take this seriously because fashion and design is my passion. I love horses and everything, but when I grow up, I am going to be a fashion designer in New York City."

That was the other thing she loved about working with kids—seeing the possibilities and potential of all the wonderful things they could do with their lives. Growing up, Josie had had all kinds of dreams, but only Brady and Abigail had encouraged her. As she saw Kayla's happiness as she described what she wanted to do, Josie's heart warmed with the knowledge that Kayla had two parents who would support her in this journey.

When Kayla was finished, Josie gave her an encouraging hug. "That all sounds wonderful. Have you told your mom about this? You should be helping her more with the costumes. It would be a great skill you could put on your résumé."

Kayla groaned and rolled her eyes. "I just get in the way, and she snaps at me about it. That's why I want to go away to New York City. I won't have her breathing down my neck all the time."

Though Josie wanted to laugh because she heard the same thing from so many teenagers, she nodded understandingly as she followed Kayla down the hall. "I know it feels that way, but your mom loves you. I wish I'd had a mom who cared about me like she does when I was growing up."

"Your mom died, didn't she?" Kayla asked.

Josie nodded. "Yes. She died giving birth to me, so I never knew her. Until recently, I didn't even know her family." She smiled as she thought about the text she had just received from her uncle Dean.

Kayla gave her a sympathetic look. "That's really sad. I guess I never thought of it that way, but I am grateful to have a mom. I just wish she'd let me do more stuff. It's so unfair."

Josie gave Kayla another squeeze. "I know it feels that way sometimes, but just remember that your mom loves you and has your best interests at heart."

As they rounded the corner toward the arena, a group of girls waved over Kayla.

"Check out this video of a new trick. We're trying to figure out if any of us can pull it off."

Kayla turned to give Josie another smile. "Thanks for talking to me. I'm going to go check out that new trick."

As Kayla scampered off, Josie said a quick prayer that her words had done some good and that Kayla would realize just how much her mom loved her. It was hard for a teenager to understand a mother's love, but it was obvious to Josie.

She watched as the girls waved over their instructor to show him the video. Their enthusiasm reminded her of when she was that age and how she and her friends got excited over the latest tricks. They might not have had the same level of social media then, but they were still looking things up on the internet, finding new tricks and huddling together over the ancient office computer.

When she turned to go back toward the office, Brady stood there, leaning against the doorway leading to the paddock and barn where the horses were kept.

"You were wonderful with Kayla just now," he said, a tender look in his eyes.

Josie shrugged. "It's normal teenager stuff. She just needs to know how much the people around her care about her."

The look Brady gave her made her want to melt all the way down to her toes. It was hard to believe he could still have that effect on her after everything they'd been through. In times like these, she was tempted to explore these feelings, but it was so hard to learn to trust again after he'd betrayed her.

"I was going to check the horses' water," he said. "Do you feel like taking a walk with me?"

She should say no, given that she was feeling all fluttery inside already. But how was she supposed to resist that charming smile?

"Sure," she said. "I've been sitting most of the day, so it'll be nice to stretch my legs."

She'd learned her lesson from her high-heel misadventure, so even though she wasn't going to let go of her need to wear pretty clothes, she'd found several more practical shoes that still looked cute with what she wore. Today she had on a sweet pair of tennis shoes that matched her dress perfectly.

As they walked, Josie could feel the stress of the day washing off her. It wasn't that she had a particularly difficult day, but it still felt soothing to be walking in the fresh air with Brady. Years ago, she thought that moments like these would be everyday occurrences with him. Having gone so long without, she was going to take the time to breathe in appreciation and send a silent prayer of thanks to God for this moment.

After they'd been walking for a few minutes, Brady said, "I know you brush off what you do as being something you've been trained for, and all of this is just normal teen stuff like with Kayla. But I hope you know that you have a very special gift."

Part of her wanted to shrug it off, but the sincere look on Brady's face made her want to acknowledge it.

"Thank you," she said. "Growing up, I felt so lost and alone, so my goal has always been to help others not feel the same."

Brady reached for her hand, and she let him take it. He stopped, squeezing her hand, then pulled her closer to him. It wasn't a full embrace, but close enough. "You're doing a great job. Things with Kayla weren't bad before you came, but I still see a positive change in her, and I know it's because you're part of her life."

The compliment warmed her deeper than she felt most compliments from parents who appreciated her work with their children. As much as she hated to admit it, her feelings stemmed a lot from how she felt about Brady and wanting to give his child special care. Kayla was a good kid with loving, supportive parents, and she was easy to love.

"Don't sell yourself short," Josie told Brady. "You've done a wonderful job with her."

Brady brought her hand up to his lips and kissed it. "That means a lot, coming from you."

Though it was just a simple brush of his lips against her fingers, it sent ripples of energy through her body. She wasn't supposed to be feeling things for him again. Despite all the times she reminded herself of this, when she looked over at him and saw the love in his eyes, she wanted to wrap her arms around him and kiss him with all the emotion that had been building up in her.

"Brady…"

She didn't know what she was trying to say, or even what she wanted to say, but he knew. He let go of her hand and stepped away. "I'm sorry. Sometimes I can't help myself. The feelings I had for you that I thought I had let go keep rushing back, and I don't know what to do about it."

If only her heart didn't remember the pain of having him cheat on her. It seemed silly to keep going back to that thought, especially since they had both changed over the years. But as Josie was still learning to exercise her forgiveness muscle, it seemed easier to forgive someone who had died than to be standing next to someone who could potentially hurt her again.

Her throat tightened as she came to this realization. Somewhere, in all of this, she was starting to forgive her father.

The Bible told her that she needed to forgive seventy times seven, and Brady had only done the one thing wrong.

Josie took a deep breath. "I have the same struggle," she admitted.

"I'm new at this forgiveness thing, and I want you to know that I am genuinely trying to forgive you. It shouldn't be that hard, and I hope that with the Lord's help, we can find a way past this. God brought us back together for a reason."

She thought about how she had made them see that saving the stables might not be God's plan, and part of their faith in God had to be about trusting Him with whatever outcome happened. Maybe it was time to give this situation to God as well.

"I keep dismissing our romantic feelings because of our past," Josie said. "But I think it's time for me to trust God with this as well. I don't know what that looks like, except to say that I'm willing to trust Him and be open to whatever happens."

Brady nodded slowly. "I want to trust in God, too. But the truth is, I'm not sure I trust myself. I still don't know why I cheated on you, and it's been keeping me up at night. If I don't understand why I did it to begin with, how can I promise you I won't do it again? I was drunk, and while that doesn't excuse it, it makes me wonder how I could have made such a terrible mistake."

He'd told her this before, but this time, as she listened to his words, something jumped out at her. "Do you still drink?"

A surprised look crossed Brady's face. "No, of course not. I learned my lesson from that one mistake. It was bad enough, waking up with my head pounding. But after I saw those pictures of me with Maddie, and all the things people were saying, I understood why we weren't supposed to drink. It turned me into a person I didn't like or recognize."

Funny how an openness to God made that one detail come out. "Would you have made that decision had you not been drinking?"

Again, Brady looked taken aback. "No. That's the whole reason my actions that night surprised me. Even that next morning, I didn't understand how I could have done what I did."

She thought about what she had learned about forgiveness, and she said a quick prayer, then asked, "And have you talked to God about it? Did you ask Him for the forgiveness of your sins?"

Brady nodded forcefully. "Yes. I spent hours on my knees, telling God how sorry I was because I understood my failing, and I thanked Him for choosing to bless me with a wonderful daughter despite my mistake."

A strange peace settled over Josie. "I—I believe you," she said slowly. "Maybe I don't quite understand the frame of mind you were in or why you made that particular decision, but I do believe that had you not been drinking that night, you would not have cheated on me. Since you haven't drunk since then, I trust you won't do it again."

The relief on his face was more freeing to her than she would have expected. But as she took a few deep breaths, silently asking God what all of this meant, she felt even more peace.

"If you say you asked God for forgiveness, then based on what we know about God and forgiveness, we know that He has forgiven you. So if God has forgiven you, and we know you aren't going to do it again, then I think it's time I forgave you, and you forgave yourself."

Brady reached forward and pulled her into a deep hug. "Thank you," he said. "You didn't tell me anything I didn't already know, but now, I believe it with all my heart."

He held her tight against him, and for the first time since being back, Josie allowed herself to settle into his embrace and feel the full force of his love for her. She had been so afraid of being hurt again that she hadn't seen a way to let herself love again, either.

And now it was time.

When Brady finally let her go, he looked at her and smiled in that way that always made her knees go weak.

"So what now?" he asked.

"I don't know," Josie said. "I guess we start over, but I'm not sure how. We still have Maddie and Kayla to think about. I don't want to rush into anything, and I think we need to take things slow so that whatever happens between us, Kayla doesn't suffer."

Brady pulled her into his arms again. "That is the best answer anyone could have given. The times I've tried dating never worked out because people didn't understand my commitment to Kayla."

"I understand that commitment." Josie looked up and smiled. "It's why I let you go in the first place."

"I know," he said. "And I love you for that. I'm excited to see what this new chapter holds for us."

He bent and kissed her. His lips were soft and gentle. Exploring but not pushing. Different and new. It truly was a kiss that said they were beginning again.

Chapter Nine

The weekend had gone by too quickly for Josie. After the kiss she'd shared with Brady, it had been a whirlwind of activity, with various projects at the stables unexpectedly popping up. They hadn't had any personal time to explore further what that kiss meant. Though it felt like movement forward, there was still a lot to work out to determine what their relationship would look like in the future. Splitting her time between Denver and Shepherd's Creek was becoming exhausting. But she'd run out of vacation time, and as much as she longed to be at the stables more, she also enjoyed her work here in Denver. That was truly the problem and the thing no one at the stables understood. She had a good life here, and she was happy.

"Do you have a minute?" Serena Fong, her coworker, asked, popping her head into Josie's office.

Josie set aside the flyer for the fundraiser she'd been looking at. Though they still had some time to go, it still felt like saving the stables was a castle in the air.

"Yes. We've got a few minutes before we meet with Alexa about the summer camp. I'm excited to see the programming everyone has been working so hard on. I think it's going to be the best one yet."

The rec department took the kids in their program on a summer campout every year. It was a great way for the city kids to experience the wilderness for themselves. For many, it would be the first time they had ever had the opportunity to sleep in a tent. This was the final planning meeting with Josie's boss, Alexa, to ensure they had everything in place.

"That's what I wanted to talk to you about," Serena said. "We usually work with Outdoor Adventures Incorporated as our provider for the horseback rides and the chuckwagon cookout."

Josie nodded. "Yes, they've been fantastic partners."

Serena tossed a stack of papers on Josie's

desk. "Not so fantastic. The owner, Michael Johnson, just got arrested for embezzlement. They're shutting down operations and selling everything off. I have a whole list of activities we can't provide, including all the horse stuff. I realize this is a big ask, but with that stables you go down to, do you have any connections to anyone who could provide enough horses to give these kids a trail ride and a chuckwagon dinner?"

A light bulb went off in Josie's head. The campsite they used was only thirty minutes from the stables. The number of horses they had available for rental was big enough to handle the campers, as well as having some in reserve, just in case.

"We'll have to get Alexa to sign off on it since there is an obvious conflict of interest with my owning the stables, but Shepherd's Creek Equestrian Complex would easily be able to handle it."

Serena grinned. "I was hoping you'd say that. I put together a list of other possibilities, but to be perfectly honest, none of them are licensed or insured to handle such a large group of children. I'm assuming Shepherd's Creek has all of that in place since they already work with kids."

That was one of the things Josie had made sure was recently updated. With everything on the line for the show, she'd wanted to be sure that no bureaucratic red tape would stand in their way. They were going to do this event, and they were going to do it right, which meant having all the proper permits and documentation. A bit more expensive and more of a headache, but she was committed to the event's success. She still didn't know if it would be enough to keep the stables open, but no one was going to be able to accuse her of not giving it her all.

In the meeting with Alexa a little while later, Serena presented the challenge of losing Outdoor Adventures Incorporated as the activity provider for their summer-camp program, then allowed Josie to share about the stables. Alexa agreed and thought that opening up a bidding process in which the bids were submitted blindly and Josie was not one of the decision makers would provide a fair opportunity for the stables and anyone else to try for the job.

For Josie, this was exactly the boon the stables needed. While they would have to go through a bidding process, the fact of the matter was, as Serena had so astutely pointed out, there weren't any other organizations that provided the same kinds of services they wanted for the camp.

Not only could Josie see the benefit to the rec department, but she also knew how this would help the stables. Even a rough mental calculation told her that it would provide consistent income to the stables, giving them the boost they needed. This, plus the fundraiser, gave her hope for the first time that maybe they could save the stables after all.

After the meeting, Josie and Serena went back to her office.

"We have to make this work," Serena said. "You weren't here back then, but when we were first looking for contractors to provide the summer activities, all of our other options were so sketchy that we almost had to cancel the summer programming. I've kept my eye out for other people because I always thought that the other place was a little too expensive. If anything, our options have gotten worse."

Josie had often had similar thoughts. Hiring them had always stretched their budget to a point that had made her uncomfortable. Serena's confirmation gave Josie more confidence in the idea of using the stables to put together the bid.

"I agree," Josie said. "I'll give Brady a call to have him get started on putting the information we need together, and then I can follow up when I'm there this weekend."

Serena stared at her for a moment, then shook her head. "I have a better idea. Why don't you go down there and make sure that everything is up to standards? We don't have anything going on that you need to be on-site this week, so take your laptop and work from the stables because this needs to be our top priority."

Everything on Josie's calendar for the week was about making their summer program successful. Today's meeting was supposed to have been about finalizing the last details. However, this plan change made finding a replacement for Outdoor Adventures Incorporated the most urgent priority.

Strange how she had been hoping for an opportunity to spend more time at the stables, but hadn't wanted to sacrifice her job. This bad turn of events could be used for good.

"That sounds like a great idea," Josie said. "I'll gather what I need to work on this week. Would you mind putting together the details that I'll need to verify for the riding program?"

As Serena nodded and left the room, Josie received a text from her uncle Dean. Since his visit to the stables, they'd touched base off and on, giving Josie insight into her family, and Dean had been very good about not pressuring her about the sale. So his invitation to lunch today brought a smile to her face. She texted her agreement, then called Brady.

"You're never going to guess what just happened," she said when he picked up.

"I haven't heard you sound that excited since you beat out Jessica Andrews for the chance at carrying the American flag for the Veteran's Day parade."

Funny how such a small thing had brought her so much joy growing up. But this was even better.

Josie gave a small laugh, then explained the newest opportunity for the stables.

"Just how much money are we talking?" Brady asked.

"I haven't run the numbers, and I need to go over some details with you, but from what I know of the budgets, both for the stables and the rec department, I'm pretty sure that the contract itself would cover our current budget deficiencies. If we can establish a long-term working relationship, this could easily put us in the black for the foreseeable future."

"Wow," Brady said. "So the fundraiser would just be gravy?"

Warmth filled Josie as she thought of how she was bringing her two passions together. "We still need the fundraiser," she said. "I'm just talking operating expenses here. You've pointed out many improvements that have to happen at the stables, and this might be a way to do it all."

She could hear Brady's smile over the phone. "This is amazing. I can't believe how everything is coming together so easily."

Josie laughed again. "Now, don't be putting your cart before the horse. As I said, I haven't run the numbers yet, and we haven't gotten the bid, either. But I'm coming home this afternoon so we can work on it. My boss is allowing me to work from home for the week so we can put together the strongest bid possible."

Brady was quiet for a moment, then he said, "Did you just refer to the stables as home?"

It had been so automatic that she hadn't realized she'd done it, but as she thought about the answer to his question, she said, "Yes, I guess I did. It is starting to feel a lot more like home, but I hope you know that this is also my home. Being here, putting together programs for the children, I truly love my work. I'm still trying to figure out how to reconcile all of that, but if the stables gets this bid, it would be a lot easier for me to do both."

She wouldn't have expected that a challenge facing her job would bring her so much peace about the frustrations and uncertainties she had been feeling about balancing everything. Could a problem be a solution? But as she reminded herself, she needed to keep her warnings to Brady in mind. That didn't stop her from sending a silent prayer to God.

I know I've said that I would be open to all possibilities, but this one feels right. If this is meant to be, please open all the doors that need to be opened, and if it's not, please don't keep our hopes up for too long. Amen.

As Josie put together the files she needed to work on while at the stables, Serena came back into her office.

"Here is the information you'll need to put together the bid." Serena handed her a folder, then hesitated. "This might be premature of me, but last year, the feedback we got about our horse activities was the best the program has seen. But we've also had such a huge waiting list that we haven't been able to accommodate everyone who wants to join. I haven't brought this up to Alexa, but could you also look at possibilities for expanding the program? We may not be able to do more of the campouts, but do you think there's any way we could do something like day trips?"

A couple of years ago, they had worked with another outfitter in another part of the state to do day-trip horseback rides. It had been wildly popular, but the company had been run by an older man who had decided to retire after only a couple of years. They hadn't been able to find a replacement, so they'd stopped that program. Which was the same direction this campout program would go if Josie's bid wasn't accepted.

Funny how so many roads for helping the rec center led back to the stables.

"I can certainly look into it."

Before the now-retired outfitter, they'd had several programs allowing city kids to experience horses using other providers. But all the stables near the city had become too expensive and beyond their budget. Josie had always thought that Shepherd's Creek Equestrian Complex was an amazing bargain, and even if they raised their prices, it was still less than anything the rec department had available to them.

"Thank you," Serena said. "I know you never thought that growing up with horses was such a big deal, but I always envied that about you. I can't even have a dog at my condo. I know I'm projecting, but the more I can do to give these kids more opportunities, the bigger difference we can make in their lives."

Months ago, Josie would have told Serena that she didn't think the stables would have provided such a great environment for the kids. But seeing how Abigail still poured herself into their lives, how Brady legitimately cared about each and every child who walked through those doors, and the tireless dedication of every instructor who volunteered their time to make things better for their riders, she was beginning to let go of her old prejudices. And, dare she say it, forgive those who had wronged her in the past.

"I'm here to do whatever we can to help the children whose paths we cross," Josie affirmed, taking the folder from Serena. "I love that we provide so much for the children we serve. There's art for the artistic ones, sports for the athletic ones, and if we can give horses to our animal lovers, that's an even larger population we can help."

Serena nodded. "Exactly. I'm not sure yet what budget we can get for this, so give me a few different options to play with."

Josie gathered her things, noting she had just enough time to stop by a dance shop close to the restaurant where she was meeting Dean. Kayla had made a PowerPoint presentation about the new costumes she wanted for her mom and sent Josie a copy. Josie was sure the dance shop would have a couple of things that might fit Kayla's vision. She could pick up a few samples and bring them back with her to the stables.

Which was why, as Josie browsed the various costume options at the dance store, she felt good about picking out something suitable for Kayla. And, after talking with the owner, she had worked out a deal to get a discount on some of their costume needs that the residents at the nursing home where Maddie worked wouldn't be able to do.

Talk about a successful day.

She knew she was beaming from ear to ear as she sat down at the restaurant with her uncle.

"Something's got you smiling," he said as he greeted her warmly.

"So many good things," she said. Then her heart sank a little as she realized that she'd likely have to deal disappointing news to him. "But I'm afraid you're not going to be happy."

He gave a half smile as he nodded slowly. "You're not going to sell me the stables, are you?"

Josie shrugged. "If everything works out the way I think it might, I won't have to. But I hate the thought that we've stood in the way of your business for so long, and here we are, doing it again."

Dean chuckled. "I'll admit that I'm always disappointed at missing out on a chance to make more money. But maybe this whole situation was orchestrated simply to bring us together. I found an old letter from your mother, apologizing for the way your father had slighted us over a holiday. In it, she said that he was never the kind of man to apologize flat out. But he always found ways to say he was sorry."

A smile filled his face as he continued. "Sure enough, a few months later, he sent us this gift basket that, to us, was a trifle and mostly meaningless. But I know how your parents were struggling financially back then, and that gift basket was probably bought with all the money he had. Your mother had said that he'd had some good rides at a few rodeos, so that must have been where he got the money from. We didn't appreciate it the way we should have and instead were offended at this meaningless gesture."

A dark expression crossed his face, then he sighed. "I wonder what would have happened if we'd seen that gift for how precious it had been to him and properly thanked him for it instead of treating it as an insult."

His story resonated with Josie because that sounded a lot like her father. Sadness filled her as she realized how many times she scoffed at his gifts that were probably the only way he knew how to say he was sorry. She'd wanted the apology, but the gift was all he'd had to give.

"I think we're all guilty of that," she said.

Were the stables the ultimate gift or the ultimate insult? The harder Josie worked to save them, the more she could see that this was probably the only way her father knew how to say he was sorry for everything. He'd already set the wheels in motion to connect her with her mother's family with the potential sale, so it was the ultimate way for him to express regret and try to right the wrongs that had haunted him at the end of his life.

Suddenly, saving the stables wasn't just about giving back to Abigail or Brady or the community in which she had grown up, but it was her way of accepting her father's apology. She'd already been working on forgiving him, but this took the process a step further.

"Thanks for sharing that story," Josie said. "It's made me realize a lot of truths about my father I haven't been willing to accept. I've been insulted when people compared my stubbornness to his, but the truth is, I have probably gotten a lot from him."

Dean laughed. "Oh, don't underestimate how much you got from your mother, too. Two stubborn people like that are bound to produce an equally stubborn child. But you have a good heart, and that's what's important."

Then he pulled an envelope out of his briefcase and handed it to her. "I suspected that you weren't going to sell, but I still want to support you. Add me to your list of sponsors. Here's a donation to show my support."

As she took the envelope, he said, "But if

things don't work out, we can talk about you selling again."

The rest of their lunch was leisurely, and it felt good to have this deepened family connection. It seemed like everything was finally coming together, and Josie couldn't help saying another prayer of thanksgiving as she left the restaurant.

On her way out, she was surprised to run into Maddie. She did a double take, then asked, "Maddie. What brings you all the way to Denver?"

Maddie glared at her. "I had to come up for a certification class, and we're just finishing our lunch break."

The tension in Maddie's voice made Josie feel sorry for her. Maybe the other woman was running late to get back to her class. "That's great," Josie said. "I don't want to keep you or make you late, but when you get back, come by the stables. I found the perfect costume for Kayla's idea."

"That's my job," Maddie said. "I'm her mother."

Josie had thought they were past this. "I'm sorry, I didn't mean to overstep. We talked about seeing what this dance store had, and it was right on my way. Kayla sent me the

PowerPoint she made for you, so I thought it would be okay to pick up a few samples. When we get back to the stables, you can take a look, and I can return anything you don't like. The best news is the dance store has agreed to give us a discount."

The grumpy expression didn't leave Maddie's face, and Josie's spirits fell. It seemed like all the progress they had made had been lost. But hopefully, once they got back to the stables, they could talk things out and everything would be fine again.

"I'm sorry," Josie said. "I'm probably making you late. Instead of coming by to approve the costume when you get home, let's have a cup of coffee or tea, and we can talk this out. I truly meant no harm, and I want to make sure we're good."

Maddie didn't answer but instead stormed away.

At this point, it would do no good to chase after her and press her further, especially if she was late getting back to her training. God had fixed worse between them, so Josie was confident that they would get through this, too.

Seeing Josie pull into the stables on a Monday afternoon was one of the most welcome sights Brady had seen in a long time. She'd only left yesterday after lunch, but even in that short time, he'd missed her. They'd kissed and decided to take their relationship in a romantic direction on Friday, but since then, they hadn't had a moment alone together. Hopefully, with her working from home this week, they could find a few stolen moments in the evenings to explore their connection further.

At times like this, when his breath was taken away at the ordinary act of her getting out of a car, he was grateful to have her back in his life. After all, the woman she had become, and was still becoming, astounded him.

"It has been the most amazing morning," Josie said, happiness radiating from her. "A little bump after lunch, but we can talk about that later. I'm assuming you're free?"

Brady gestured at the barn. "My weekly meeting with all the volunteers is getting ready to start. Why don't you join us, and if you don't think it's premature, you can tell them about the opportunity to partner with the rec center. Maybe they have information or ideas that could help in your proposal."

Josie hesitated. "I don't want to get anyone's hopes up."

Then she squared her shoulders. "However, the rec department needs this as badly as we do, and from the research we've already done, Shepherd's Creek stables is their only hope as well. So if we could put together something really special, it could be a win for all of us."

His heart ached at the enthusiasm in her voice. Not because there was anything wrong with what she had said, but because what he wanted most was to take her in his arms, hold her tight, tell her how proud he was of her and then kiss her.

They'd taken a new step in their relationship Friday afternoon, and now, he was aching to find out more about the woman he was falling back in love with.

But as had happened all weekend, the priority was figuring out how they could make their plans for the stables work. His heart would have to wait.

"Then let's get in there and see what we can do," he said.

He'd set the meeting for the main arena, in the center stands, so they could have a better picture of what the show would be like. Josie took her seat with the volunteer leadership committee, and Brady took the podium to greet everyone. It seemed like everybody was there, except Maddie, but she had told him that she would be late if she could come at all, because she had a certification class in Denver.

Though he would have liked everyone to be in attendance, it was hard to work around people's schedules. But with his and Josie's relationship with Maddie improved so significantly over the last few weeks, he wasn't worried about not sharing the most recent developments with her now. There would be plenty of time for the three of them to discuss, and it felt good to be on the same page as Maddie finally.

As Brady went through the agenda, he was pleased to hear how each committee member was right on track with all the tasks they had been assigned for the fundraiser. As he looked at all the bright, shining faces of various people, most of whom he'd known his whole life, he felt an incredible blessing at the knowledge of how all these people had come together for the sake of their community.

When it came time for people to report in about any additional sponsorships they'd received, Josie stood, a broad smile on her face.

"I have a new sponsorship to share. The Islington Holdings company gave us the platinum-level sponsorship, and with this do-nation, we have exceeded our sponsorship goal. Bravo, everyone."

As the group gathered in the stands burst into applause, Brady's heart swelled with pride. Though Josie hadn't told him how the sponsorship came about, he could only as-sume that it meant they had withdrawn their offer to buy the stables and were instead look-ing to support the endeavor. Which wouldn't surprise him, since Josie had spent a lot of time talking to her uncle and getting to know that side of the family. They obviously be-lieved in her as much as Brady did.

"Wait just one second," Maddie said, com-ing around the side of the bleachers and strid-ing to the podium. "Don't you be applauding that blood money. Islington Holdings is the development company who's buying the sta-bles to tear it down and put in tract homes, exactly what we're supposed to be stopping."

Gasps echoed through the audience. Mad-die carried a poster board, which she held up.

"Anyone recognize this?"

The audience murmured because they ob-viously did.

The drawings showed a housing development on a familiar piece of property—where the stables sat.

"I talked to the county, and I have copies of all the studies Islington Holdings has done on our area over the years. This isn't the first time they've tried to ruin our community. Anyone remember when we had to fight the developers and create the nature sanctuary? These are the same monsters. These are the people Josie is selling the stables to."

Brady took a deep breath and said a quick prayer before looking over at Josie.

"I'm sure there's a misunderstanding," he said. "Josie has been talking to them, yes, but she's not selling."

"I saw her meeting with them today," Maddie said. "This isn't the first time I've seen her with Dean Islington, the CEO. They met at a restaurant in the same building as the architectural firm that drew up these plans. I saw him giving her the documents."

"That's not what you saw," Josie said. "They're giving us a sponsorship. The envelope you saw him giving me was the signed sponsorship agreement from our website, along with a check. He's helping us."

Maddie shook the poster board. "That's not what this says. Permits have been filed. I don't know what kind of scam you people are pulling, but why would he file for permits if you weren't selling?"

Brady's heart thundered in his chest as he remembered the last public confrontation between Maddie and Josie. It had been at the stables' Christmas party, all those years ago, when Maddie accused Josie of spreading rumors about her being pregnant, then triumphantly announced that they were true for once and that Brady was the father.

As he watched the crumpled expression on Josie's face, he could tell that she remembered, too. Back then, Brady had been too shell-shocked to go to Josie, but this time, in his heart, he knew this had to be a big misunderstanding, and where he hadn't been able to support her before, he was going to support her now.

He strode over to Josie and put his arm around her. "Josie told me this morning about a plan to save the stables that doesn't involve selling them. That was going to be the next thing we talked about today. We're all in this together, so whatever you found that proves that there is a sale, there's got to be a misunderstanding. I choose to believe Josie, and we'll get to the bottom of the situation."

He felt Josie relax under his touch. "I've signed no contract," Josie said. "Brady is right. The plan I wanted to share with all of you won't just save the stables, but I believe that it will make it better than ever."

Maddie ripped one of the papers off the poster board and strode over to them, waving it in Josie's face. "This is an application for a development permit. You don't put one of those in without an intent to build on the land."

Brady took it out of her hand. "We will examine it in due time. But Josie has just told all of us that she's committed to saving the stables, and rather than making all these public accusations, let's go back and figure out what's going on here."

"I saw her hugging the developer. Not just today, but a couple of months ago, when she took him on a tour of the property. Since then, I have been investigating the activities of the development company, and it's very clear that they intend to build here. She's in on their plans."

Things were just getting messier and messier. Brady wished Maddie would stop with the public confrontation and sit down with them and all her evidence. But this was how Maddie did things and why dealing with her was so difficult at times.

"So that's why you were upset with me earlier today," Josie said. "I wish you had just come to me with all of this. Dean Islington is my uncle. That's why I was hugging him. Before his death, my father contacted my uncle Dean, my mother's brother, partially to sell the stables, but I also believe to heal the rift between him and my mother's family after my mother died. Yes, Dean would love to develop this property. But—"

"Don't *but* us," Maddie screeched. "I'm so tired of your fake attitude, your lies and your whole pretend-forgiveness thing. This is just like when we were in high school, and you invited me to that campout where you all humiliated me by encouraging me to pitch a tent on an anthill."

More of the old drama from their past. By the frozen expression on Josie's face, he could tell that she remembered. It was one more misunderstanding between Maddie and Josie, and even though Brady had always believed in Josie's innocence in that situation as well, convincing Maddie was another story.

"We're never going to get anywhere if you keep bringing up the past," Josie said. "I know because I am trying so hard to move on and find forgiveness and resolution of my own past. I am truly sorry for what happened between us as kids, but none of that is relevant now."

She gestured at the audience members, who were murmuring among themselves. Judging from the overall confusion, Brady was pretty sure they didn't know what to believe, and he could understand. What was happening here had nothing to do with them, but Maddie was making them a part of it.

"If any permits were issued," Josie said, "I have no knowledge of it. But I can assure you, I will get to the bottom of everything."

Then she turned to the audience. "I'm sorry that you all had to be dragged into this. I know I have only recently returned and that when I first came back, I was not committed to the stables. But having been back and reconnected with all of you, saving the stables is an important priority in my life."

Maddie looked like she was going to start trouble again and was digging in her bag like she had more evidence of Josie's wrongdoing. Maddie could produce all the evidence she needed, but it wouldn't shake Brady's unwavering faith in Josie.

Josie squared her shoulders as she continued addressing the audience. "As many of you know, I work for a recreation center in Denver. As part of our summer programming, we take the kids on an annual camping trip, where they have the opportunity to also spend time with horses. Unfortunately, our usual contractor is not able to help us this year. I'm here to put together a proposal to take back to the rec center so that Shepherd's Creek stables will be the new horseback-ride provider for the rec center. We have some work to do, but I'm confident we can win the bid, and if we win the bid, along with our fundraiser, Shepherd's Creek stables has a long solid future ahead of it."

Brady could see that the audience was slowly coming around to Josie. But he also saw the familiar rage building up in Maddie.

"I've talked to Josie about this proposal," Brady said, nodding at Josie. "And I agree with her. We have an excellent opportunity to make a difference in this community and to bring the world we love to children who wouldn't otherwise experience it. As Josie said, we have some work to do, but I know that if we all work together, we can succeed."

Maddie pulled a document out of her bag.

"I have the signed contract right here. Josie is going to sell."

"I never signed a contract," Josie insisted, her face getting red with what Brady knew was the exertion of trying not to cry.

Brady grabbed Maddie by the arm. "That's enough. I told you we would look at all those documents later because I'm sure there is a rational explanation for everything. Since you can't seem to wait until we can go through this as adults, you are no longer welcome in this meeting."

He turned to Josie. "Please continue. Explain to them what you're doing with the rec center and how it will benefit the stables, and why, at this point, selling would ruin everything for both your rec center and our stables."

Josie gave him a jerky nod as he glared at Maddie to get her out of the arena. He'd feared she'd put up more of a fight, but she went with him, and he didn't say a word until they arrived in his office and shut the door behind them.

Chapter Ten

Josie stood at the podium, shaking. None of these people had any reason to believe her, especially because Maddie claimed to have evidence otherwise.

"I'm truly sorry that my personal issues are getting in the way here," Josie said after offering a silent prayer that God would give her the words that she needed.

"I don't know what evidence Maddie says she has, but I have never signed any contracts agreeing to sell the stables. I remember all of the things I loved about this community, and I'm not going to let the stables go without a fight."

She looked around the audience for a friendly face, but all she saw were frowns and looks of concern. She supposed she didn't blame them, considering she hadn't come home with the best of attitudes. But even if they didn't believe her now, hopefully, she would find a way to win them over.

Hal, her father's old friend, stood. "It sounds like you have some investigating to do. I believe you, but I also believe Maddie. We all want what's best for both the community and the stables. We've all been given our jobs and will continue with our assignments. I think we should take a break now and reconvene when everything is settled. We can discuss this at next week's meeting."

Though it wasn't a glowing round of support, at least she was being given a chance to prove herself. As the community members shuffled out, Josie smiled at them, hoping she provided a reassuring presence, but inside, she felt the familiar frustration and confusion as she remembered the last time she and Maddie had publicly gone toe-to-toe. It had been at the stables' annual Christmas party, and she and Maddie had argued over something ridiculous. Then, because she hadn't given Maddie whatever answer it was that Maddie was expecting, Maddie publicly accused her of spreading rumors about her, which Josie hadn't done. Josie had never gotten the opportunity to prove her innocence because instead, Maddie had announced to everyone that the rumors were true. Worse, though, Maddie had told everyone that she was pregnant with Brady's baby.

This was that same sickening feeling, where deep in her heart, Josie knew that she was innocent. But rather than being able to prove her innocence, she worried Maddie had something on her so terrible that Josie's guilt or innocence wouldn't matter.

Hal was the last to leave. He walked over to her and hugged her. "It'll all work out. I know you and Maddie have bad blood, but I've also seen how the two of you have been working together to get over it. Forgiveness is never a linear process, even though we make it sound that way. This is just a bump in the road, and all will be well."

Though it felt good to have his arms comforting her, and it was nice to have those words, Josie felt the old familiar fear rising inside her. She'd remembered how, before the big public fight at the Christmas party, after Maddie had confronted her in the restroom, Josie had broken down in tears and prayed, asking God to be her deliverer.

But she wasn't delivered, except into a

nightmare, where she'd found out that the man she'd trusted the most had betrayed her in the worst way.

She'd barely rediscovered her faith, and now she was facing a similar crisis, where she knew she needed God to get her through it, but she wasn't sure if she was going to like His answer.

But she remembered what Brady had told her, reflecting her advice from the days long ago, when she had reminded him that faith wasn't about God giving you whatever you wanted, but about the communication and relationship with Him.

Could she trust God to bring her through this, even if she didn't like His answer?

When Hal left, Josie looked around the arena, remembering the good things that had happened there. She also noticed the way things had improved. The opposite stands had been freshly cleaned, and the walls repainted. As she surveyed the area she realized the work they'd done over the last few months had made it almost unrecognizable from its previous shabby appearance.

Hanh Nguyen, who owned the local hardware store, had donated paint and other supplies they needed for the repairs. Many of the parents had come out before and after the rides to help. And Brady had started a program where the families who couldn't pay their rent would donate a certain number of hours in lieu of the fees.

Because of those efforts, the stables looked better than ever, and she hoped that when people came to see the show, they would see a place they wanted to bring their families to. Maybe, as had always been her father's goal with his performances, it would be a good recruiting tool for those coming to watch. Finally, as she looked around the place, what she saw was hope.

When they had prayed all those weeks ago, Josie and Brady had agreed that they would follow God wherever He took them. She couldn't see how, when she had so much hope that everything would be okay, this would all be for nothing. Even though past evidence had told her that those prayers didn't work out for her the way she'd planned, she still wanted to believe in God's goodness and provision.

She closed her eyes and prayed. *Please, God, I don't know what's going to happen. And I don't know what to make of all the evidence Maddie has against me. But I'm trying*

*to believe in Your good plan, so please, show
me the way out.*

Usually, Josie felt better after praying, but
this one didn't leave her with a feeling of
peace. Maybe it was because of all the worries still turning in her stomach, despite handing it over to God.

That's the thing no one told you about
prayer, and Josie was still trying to figure
out. Sometimes, you get an instant answer or
at least an immediate sense of relief. But other
times, like now, as the sense of dread settled deeper into her stomach, she didn't have
a clear answer. As she walked back toward
Brady's office to find out what was going on,
her prayer hadn't changed anything inside
her, and she was moving forward slowly on
faith that God was working behind the scenes
for the good of all involved.

When she got to Brady's office, the door
was ajar, and she could hear Maddie crying.

"You've always sided with her. I've given
you evidence, and despite that, you're still
telling me to give her a chance."

She couldn't fully hear Brady's response,
but then Maddie said, with a shrill tone to her
voice, "Just stop. She's still in love with you,
and she's trying to break up our family. She

admitted to me today that she was out buying a costume for Kayla. That's my job. She's trying to take over."

Now it was just getting ridiculous. Josie entered Brady's office.

"That wasn't my intention," she said. "I thought you would be happy that I had taken the time. But as I told you earlier today, you have final approval, and it can be returned. I've already apologized for overstepping. So how else can I make this up to you?"

Maddie just glared at her.

"See?" Brady said. "There is a reasonable explanation. Just like with these documents you're showing me."

"There you go again, taking her side. I know you're still in love with her. That's why I couldn't marry you. I always knew that someday she'd come back, come between us and try to take Kayla away from me. She's all Kayla talks about anymore. Don't think I haven't noticed that Kayla's been spending way more time here than she has at home."

Josie wanted to remind Maddie that Kayla was spending all her time at the arena because she was practicing for a show. But at this point, she wasn't sure anything she could say would get through to the other woman. But she had to try.

"I would think that after our talk about how we both felt isolated as girls, that you would know I would never do anything to jeopardize Kayla's relationship with you, her mother."

Maddie started to cry. "I wanted to believe that, and you had me fooled. But I can see it plain as day. Just like every other woman who has tried to date Brady. They think they know how to be a better mother to my daughter than I can. Well, they're wrong. And you're wrong."

Though Josie knew that this was simply Maddie's insecurities coming out, it was still hard to hear. None of it was true.

"Protecting Kayla's interests is why I haven't dated much," Brady said. "I know you and Shandra had issues when we were dating, and that's why I broke things off with her. There is nothing more important to me than Kayla's best interests."

A regretful look crossed his face as he glanced over at Josie, then back at Maddie. "As far as my relationship with Josie goes, that's private between us, but I can assure you that if things were ever to become serious, we would work together to ensure that

Kayla comes first. I made you that commitment from the moment I knew I was going to be a father, and I will always keep that commitment to you and our daughter."

Even though they were in the middle of a conflict with Maddie, it felt good to have Brady on her side. If they could work through this together, it gave Josie hope that they could have a lasting relationship. Otherwise, the kiss they'd shared would be their last. Josie had always prioritized Kayla's well-being over her desire to be with Brady, and that would never change.

"Stop lying," Maddie said. "I know you two are back together. I saw you kissing on Friday. How am I supposed to believe anything either of you says when you can't even be honest with me about that?"

Though they had been in a public place, Josie had thought that it was a secluded enough location that they'd had some privacy. But apparently not. It was a little embarrassing to know that others had observed their first kiss, but also that it had been so misinterpreted by Maddie.

"How have I lied to you?" Brady asked. "I told you that my relationship with Josie was private and that if it got serious, we would work together to make sure that Kayla comes first. That's the truth. The kiss we shared, that's part of what I said was private."

Maddie squared her shoulders. "Then maybe you shouldn't have done it in a public place. If I saw, who else do you think saw?"

Josie took a deep breath. "You're right. We picked a bad place for our first kiss. Though I understand Brady wanting to keep our relationship private, I have nothing to hide from you. Ask me anything, and I'll tell you the truth."

Though Josie had been the target of Maddie's rage before, she wasn't expecting the pure hate in the other woman's eyes when she turned her gaze on Josie.

"With all the evidence I have about you working to sell the stables, why would I believe anything you have to say?" Maddie's eyes filled with tears.

Before Josie could defend herself, Maddie continued. "As for Brady's claims about putting Kayla first, oh, I believe that. Just not in the way you say. You're trying to swoop in and undermine me so the three of you can be a happy family, leaving me without my daughter."

Where was all this coming from? Tears

filled Josie's eyes as she realized this was everything she had been trying to avoid.

"No," Josie said. "After everything we've talked about regarding the importance of having a mother, I can't believe you would even accuse me of that. Everything I've said or done with Kayla has been to affirm you as a good mother."

Maddie's face grew even redder. "Lies. You two were talking in the barn the other day about Kayla's frustration with me, and you were oh, so sympathetic about the fact that Kayla didn't like my choice in costumes. And then today, you go behind my back and buy her a new costume."

How was this happening? Josie wanted to cry and scream in frustration, but that wouldn't solve anything. Back when they were kids, Josie would have walked away, unable to deal with Maddie's unwillingness to see the truth. But there was more at stake here than just their hurt feelings.

"That wasn't my entire conversation with Kayla," Josie said. "Yes, I sympathize with the fact that she didn't like the costume options, but I also encouraged her to go to you and share her ideas because I thought they were good, but ultimately you have the final say. And, as I've been trying to explain, my dance-store purchase was only an example to use as a prototype for what Kayla designed in her PowerPoint."

"What PowerPoint?" Maddie asked, raising her voice. "Just another lie you're telling to make yourself look better even though you know in your heart that you're in the wrong."

This was hopeless. Josie closed her eyes and asked God to please help them. All of this was a misunderstanding, and while Josie could see where Maddie would be genuinely hurt that she was trying to take Maddie's place in Kayla's life, that wasn't what was going on.

"That's enough," Brady said. "I have always put Kayla's best interests first, and I'm not going to stop simply because I've found someone that I could love. You're Kayla's mother, and I have always stressed to every woman who has come into my life that I will do everything possible to maintain a good relationship with you."

Even though Brady used his authoritative voice that made most people pay attention, Maddie only cried harder. "Stop lying. You're both trying to take my daughter away, just like you're secretly ruining the stables. I wouldn't be surprised if you sell the stables for a lot of money, then move away somewhere wonderful, taking Kayla with you. Well, that's not going to happen. You're not even Kayla's real father, and if I have to go to court to keep you from taking her, I will."

Speechless, Brady stared at Maddie, her words echoing in his mind. At last, he said, "What do you mean I'm not Kayla's real father?"

Maddie squared her shoulders at him defiantly, the way she always did when they argued. It meant she wasn't going to back down, and usually, in the interest of keeping the peace for Kayla's sake, Brady always gave in.

"Since the truth about everything else is coming out, I might as well tell you this truth. You aren't Kayla's father. I lied."

His heart felt tight in his chest as her words thundered over him. "I don't understand," he finally said.

"I lied," Maddie shouted. "I was mad that Josie figured out I was pregnant and was spreading rumors about me, so I thought I would get back at her by saying you were the father. Only everyone believed me, and everything snowballed until it was too late."

It was as if a dagger had been plunged into his chest.

Josie whispered, "All this because you were mad at me for something I didn't do?"

"How do you know I'm not the father? We never did a paternity test."

Maddie laughed, an evil sound that shook him to the core. "We never slept together. It was all a big joke. A couple of us thought it would be funny to play a prank on you and make you think we had, and it just snowballed."

He never slept with Maddie. Two of the most foundational events in his life weren't true. Before he could respond, a quiet whimper came from outside the door. He knew that sound.

"Kayla?" he asked softly.

Kayla stepped into the doorway, her eyes glistening. "You were all fighting about me? Why?"

Tears streamed down her face as she looked at Maddie. "Is it true? You've been lying about who my father was all this time?"

Maddie turned white as a sheet. "Oh, no. What have I done?"

"I hate you," Kayla said, looking directly at Maddie. "Dad has always been the better parent, and now you've ruined it. Josie never tried to take your place, but I wish she had. She'd make a much better mother than you."

Kayla turned and ran out of the room, leaving everyone staring after her.

"What should we do now?" Maddie said, sobbing. "I didn't mean it."

Brady stared at her, trying to ignore the disgust welling up in him. "Didn't mean what?" he asked, spitting out the words, but before she could answer, he said, "We'll figure that out later. I may not be her biological father, but Kayla is my daughter in every other way, and I'm going to find her and do what I can to make things right with her. Take me to court if you want, but I will never stop fighting for my daughter."

Brady ran out of the room and into the main barn, not caring what Maddie was feeling right now. The words she'd spoken in anger had hurt the person he loved the most in this world, and he had to make things right with his daughter.

All this time, he'd worked so hard to keep the peace with Maddie, and for what? Maddie had been harboring a terrible secret, one that had hurt them all.

He glanced around, but he didn't see Kayla

anywhere. A couple of the volunteers were standing near the paddock entrance talking.

"Did you see Kayla go by?" he asked.

Susan Walsh, who worked with the younger kids, said, "She went toward the stalls. She looked pretty upset. Is everything okay?"

Brady took a deep breath. Maddie had already caused a lot of trouble by airing her grievances against Josie and this potential sale of the stables, but the last thing he needed was for more of their private arguments to be made public. With news like this, it was inevitable people would hear of it soon enough. But he had to find his daughter first.

"Just teenager stuff," he said. "But I do need to find her and reassure her. Thank you for your help."

He noticed Maddie and Josie on his heels as he ran toward the stables. He didn't want Maddie there, and Josie, well, he didn't know what to think of having her around. His heart needed her comfort, but having her back is what caused all of this in the first place. No, not Josie. Maddie's jealousy of Josie.

The stables were empty, but Brady knew Kayla's go-to when she was upset. She was probably in the stall with her horse, crying her eyes out. Sensing Josie behind him, he remembered how she'd always done the same thing.

But when he got to Jasper's stall, it was empty.

"Looks like she took Jasper for a ride," he told the two women standing behind him.

He walked out the stable doors and looked toward the arena, but they weren't there. Instead, he could see a trail of dust in the distance. Kayla was riding hard, headed out toward open space and the national forest.

"What do we do?" Maddie asked, her face red from crying.

"Maybe you should have thought of that before blurting out such a terrible secret in anger." Though Brady knew it was wrong for him to lash out at Maddie when they were both trying to help their daughter, he also couldn't believe how they'd gotten here.

Maddie started to cry again. "I'm so sorry. I didn't mean it."

"Was it the truth?" Brady asked quietly.

Maddie nodded slowly.

Though Brady wished this was just a nightmare from which he would wake up, he knew it was real. Though he had so many questions, so many things weighing on his heart, the only thing he could think to pray was *Please, God*.

"Is there a special place she likes to ride to?" Josie asked. "We could all saddle up and head that way."

Then she took a step back. "I mean, you two could go. I'm sorry for everything I've done that has made you think I was overstepping. You're her parents, and I'll leave it to the two of you to work things out."

Then she turned to Brady, the expression on her face heartbreaking. "Hurting Kayla was the last thing I ever wanted. I know we talked about trying to make things work, but you and Maddie need to fix things with Kayla right now. I'd just be in the way. And maybe that's how it will always be."

Brady wanted to stop Josie as she walked away, but deep in his heart, he knew she was right. He'd done everything he could to make Maddie feel comfortable with his growing affection for Josie, but here they were, and somehow, Brady had to figure out a way to fix the broken pieces enough to continue having a relationship with his daughter.

Without looking at Maddie, Brady turned toward the stables. "I'm going to saddle Chief and see if I can find her. There's a place we like to ride to and have picnics at, and she's headed in that direction. Hopefully, that's where she's going."

"Brady, I'm sorry," Maddie said, her voice quivering.

Unleashing the anger he felt toward her wasn't going to bring back their daughter, so he turned and said quietly, "Now is not the time. I need to find our daughter and let her know that, despite your ugly words in there, I will always be her father."

Chapter Eleven

Though what Josie wanted most to do was crawl into bed and cry her eyes out the way she had when Maddie had announced her pregnancy, Josie had bigger things to deal with. Maddie's outburst hadn't just caused problems with Kayla, but there was still an entire community of volunteers who thought that Josie was planning on selling the stables.

Just as Maddie had misinterpreted Josie's actions and conversation with Kayla, Josie was sure that the proof that she was selling the stables had also been misunderstood. Now to find that proof, as well as a rational explanation for it.

Fortunately, when Josie went back into Brady's office, the papers Maddie had shown the volunteer committee as evidence had fallen to the floor when they'd all run out. As she gathered them, she caught the scents of fresh leather, coffee and Brady's cologne.

Her throat tightened as she inhaled the aroma of the man she'd finally allowed herself to love but couldn't have.

Her hand landed on what looked like a contract, stating the intent to sell. This must have been what Maddie was referring to. She sat on the floor examining the paper until she got to the signature. Joseph Stephen Shepherd. Her father. He always did a little squiggly at the end of his last name, and if someone wasn't looking closely, she could see where it looked like a "Junior." But that was the proof she needed. When Josie left home, changing her name hadn't just been about what people called her—she had also taken the legal steps to change it from Joseph Stephen Shepherd Junior to simply Josie Shepherd. This wasn't her signature, which meant the evidence Maddie had found was when her father was making arrangements to sell that hadn't yet been finalized.

As she pulled out her phone to call Brady, a text from him came through. She's not where I thought she'd be. No sign of her on the trails. Kayla didn't follow any safety protocol, so I'm worried about her. It's been two hours. You haven't seen her, have you?

Josie took a deep breath and said what must have been the one hundredth prayer for Kayla's safety before texting back, No.

Tears filled her eyes again as she thought about that poor girl out there, feeling so helpless and unloved. If only she'd done a better job at keeping her distance and her heart guarded against Brady. She'd thought that she and Maddie were doing so well, but clearly, a lifetime of grudges couldn't be so easily overcome.

She had to trust Brady would find Kayla. While he continued the search, she could work on saving the stables. It would be a good distraction. When the dust settled from today's mess, Josie needed to figure out a way to reestablish trust with both Maddie and the community. She hadn't done anything wrong, but here she was, once again fighting to preserve her integrity.

At least the document she found would help with that.

She called her uncle to find out what he knew of the details Maddie had shared, and as she'd suspected, it was all a misunderstanding. Preliminary paperwork had been filed as an exploratory measure, but nothing was final.

Now to find Kayla safe.

Her phone rang. Brady.

"Any news?"

"No." Brady sounded exhausted, which was understandable, given the circumstances. "She's never run off like this. Though we've been on the trails hundreds of times, she went straight to open space, so she's on unfamiliar and undeveloped terrain, which can be dangerous with all the hills and ravines. Doubly so if she's upset and not paying attention to what's around her. I hate to ask, but I need you to do me a favor. My buddy Ken, who works for the sheriff's department, volunteered to organize a search party for Kayla. Can you make sure he gets what he needs?"

"Of course. I may have chosen to step back to allow your family the chance to figure out what you all need, but that doesn't mean I've stopped caring about Kayla. I'm happy to do whatever is needed to bring her home safely."

"Thank you." He hesitated for a moment, then said, "I'm sorry for how this all turned out. I hope you understand. Kayla has to be number one."

Josie's heart ached at the pain in his voice.

Brady was dealing with so much, it hardly seemed fair that he had to worry about her feelings, too.

"I do understand," she reassured him. "We both knew there was a risk in getting involved. Focus on Kayla and doing what you need to heal your family. I'll be fine."

He was quiet for a moment, then he said, "All right. Ken knows how to find me with any updates, but I'm going to stay out here looking for my daughter until she's found. It's going to be dark soon, and I need to get her home safe."

Josie hung up the phone, then went out to the front of the stables to meet Brady's friend when he got there. Her heart was heavy, and even though she wanted to believe, like all the other disasters she faced, that God had a plan with all of this, it was frustrating that she couldn't see it.

But she had to trust and have faith. If she'd learned anything from the pain of the tragedies in her life, it was that God did have a plan, even if she didn't understand what it was until many years later. And even then, she wasn't sure she could fully know. After all, she'd just begun to deal with the upside of Brady's betrayal, only to find out that he hadn't betrayed her at all. What was God trying to teach them? She didn't know, but as she dug deeper into God's word and reestablished her relationship with Him, she knew that she had to trust and have faith regardless.

A truck pulled up and a tall man got out. "I'm Ken Pineda. Brady said you'd be expecting me."

Josie nodded. "Yes. Whatever we can provide is at your disposal."

A couple more trucks pulled up, and the men began unloading ATVs like they were already getting set for the search operation.

"We have a few ATVs, but it would be helpful if you would be willing to let us use some of your horses," Ken said. "I rounded up as many people as I could find to come help. This isn't like Kayla, and Brady is right to be worried. The sooner we find her, the better."

"Absolutely," Josie said. "Let's get your riders lined up, and we can sort out appropriate mounts for them."

As the men assembled, Josie talked to Aaron Schultz, their head wrangler, to get him working on finding the right animals for each rider. Before they had everyone on horseback, Josie noticed several vehicles pulling into the parking lot. One of the first people on the scene was Myrna Smeathers from church.

"I heard the call on the police scanner," Myrna said. "I called everyone at church and asked them to help out. I know Kayla is a fine horsewoman, but sometimes she's braver than she is smart, and if she's out there alone in the wilderness, any number of things can happen."

Within minutes, community members were organizing volunteers for the search. They'd set up a command center in the conference room, and even though Josie hated the reason they were doing it, it also warmed her heart to know that the stables were being used as another way to serve their community.

She saw Maddie in the melee, but Josie gave her a wide berth. The last thing they needed was to have their conflict interfere with such an important operation. Once everyone had their mounts, Josie looked over at the remaining horses. Perchibald, the gentle bay gelding she had been riding to get back in the saddle, was still available.

Since they had a deputy and other volunteers coordinating efforts in the conference room, Josie wasn't needed, so she went and saddled him. Noticing that the volunteers had gone in the direction of Tumbleweed Wash,

Josie decided to set out for the Big Spur picnic area. It had many quiet places where Josie had found comfort as a teenager. It was close enough to the stables and the other trails they often used that it was possible Kayla could have gone there.

She gave her location to the deputy and set off. It felt good to be on horseback, the wind in her hair, breathing in the fresh air. If only Maddie could understand the sincerity in her heart as she shared these experiences. Josie's determination to save the stables only grew with every passing moment.

The picnic area was empty when Josie arrived, but as she looked around, she remembered all the wonderful times she'd had there. After thanking God for giving her these reminders of her happiness, she also asked Him once more to keep Kayla safe.

Josie's phone buzzed at her hip, so she pulled it out and checked the text from Brady.

Kayla is safe.

She took a deep breath and said a prayer of thanksgiving. Since time was no longer of the essence, and Josie wanted to give Maddie a wide berth, she decided to take an old trail home, a longer way, but a beautiful path that would be well lit by the moonlight, given that the sun had almost set.

As she walked her horse along the trail, Josie felt some stress ease off her shoulders. God had answered her biggest prayer today, and even though she accepted that God might not answer the rest of her prayers favorably, she was grateful that this one, at least, was the response she'd wanted.

As she turned the bend, she heard a hoarse cry for help.

She gave Perchibald a tap, moving him in the direction of the sound. A few yards off the trail, she saw a person sitting in the dark. When she got closer, she recognized that person with a sinking feeling in her stomach. Maddie.

"What happened?" Josie asked when she got close enough to Maddie to talk to her.

"My horse spooked at a deer running past and threw me. I dropped my phone, so I couldn't call for help." Maddie started to cry. "I just want to find my daughter."

At least Josie could make her feel better on this account. "I just got a text that they found her safe. Kayla is okay."

"Thank God for that," Maddie said, her

tears turning to sobs. "I've messed everything up so badly, and I don't know what to do. But the worst thing is, who finds me out here, but you? Just go. If you don't hate me too much, you can send someone else to rescue me."

Josie prayed for wisdom, hoping they could find some way forward in this terrible situation.

"Are you injured?" Josie asked.

Maddie shook her head. "Just my pride."

Josie sent a quick text to the emergency coordinator, letting her know that Maddie had been thrown from her horse and they'd need help. Then she got off Perchibald and tied him to a nearby tree.

Maybe Josie was foolish for trying, but perhaps this was an opportunity from God for her and Maddie to work things out for good.

"I truly am sorry for everything that's happened between us," Josie said. "I know you don't trust me, but I promise you, every bad thing that you said about me in there is based on a misunderstanding."

Maddie glared at her. "I have no reason to trust you."

They were never going to get anywhere. But then Josie remembered the document that supposedly proved Josie's wrongdoing.

"You know that signed contract that you said is evidence that I was selling the stables?"

Maddie continued to glare up at her. "Yes. It's the smoking gun. I wanted to believe you were sincere in not wanting to sell, but about a week after I saw the investor at the stables, Kayla came home with a legal pad she'd borrowed from the office to practice her calligraphy, and the contract fell out from between the pages."

At least now she knew where the contract had been. She'd gone through all the files trying to find it, and she'd finally given up, figuring it had accidentally gotten mixed up with something else. It had, and in the worst possible way.

"You're wrong about my sincerity. But you're absolutely right about the smoking gun."

Josie squared her shoulders as she looked down at Maddie. "Ten years ago, I legally changed my name to Josie Shepherd. That document was signed by Joseph Stephen Shepherd, my father. That's not my signature, but his."

She waited while Maddie processed her words. "But there's a 'Junior' at the end."

Josie shook her head. "No, there's not. If you look at my father's official signature on everything, he does this weird little squiggly thing at the end that could be mistaken for a 'Junior,' but I would have never signed that document in that way. If you like, I can show you all of the paperwork establishing me as Josie Shepherd."

"But all the other documents?"

"I checked with my uncle. First of all, that contract was signed the day before my father died, but my father never gave it to my uncle. If you didn't carefully check the date, I can see that it would have looked like I could have signed it. The other documents you saw, yes, plans were in motion with the planning department, but my father started those plans, not me."

Maddie sniffled and wiped her sleeve across her face. "Why would he do this?"

"No one knows," Josie said. "I suspect, though, based on my conversations with my uncle, he felt bad about all the rifts in our family, and this was his way of making it up. I wish he'd lived long enough to tell us."

As strange as it sounded, she did wish her father was still alive. It would have been nice to talk to him about these things, then maybe even find their way back to having common ground.

"But you hated him."

Josie took a deep breath and said another prayer. "I did. But thanks to God's mercy and being here, I have learned to forgive him. Just like I thought we had learned to forgive each other. We still have a lot of difficulties to overcome, but I truly want restoration in my relationship with you."

The scowl on Maddie's face made Josie think she was asking the impossible.

"You're just still trying to win Brady back," Maddie said.

"No," Josie said. "Knowing how insecure my relationship with Brady and Kayla makes you feel, I'm choosing to step away. I know the three of you have lots to work out, and I don't want to impede that. As I have always said, Kayla is the most important thing here."

Maddie straightened. "You'd give Brady up? This isn't a trick?"

Clearly, Josie and her family weren't the only stubborn people in her life.

"Yes. My goal right now is to save the stables. I have to work with Brady, but I will do my best to keep our relationship on a business level. We've both agreed."

Then she remembered the misunderstanding about the costume. "As for Kayla, I promise I have done nothing to encourage her to disrespect you. Every conversation I've had with her has been affirming to you. You must have misheard our conversation about the costumes because I encouraged her to talk to you. She sent me a copy of the PowerPoint she made for you."

"What PowerPoint?"

Josie pulled out her phone, opened the app with her email, found the PowerPoint and handed it to Maddie. "This."

Maddie stared at it for a second, then said, "I haven't seen this."

She went over to Maddie and pointed at the forwarding information. "See? She forwarded me what she sent you."

Maddie read it, then let out a long sigh as she shook her head. "That's my personal email. I'm so busy with my work email that I don't often check my personal email."

She stared at the email, obviously reading what Kayla had sent Josie. Nothing special, just Kayla's excitement at having taken Josie's advice to share her passion with her mother because she trusted Josie's word that Maddie loved her daughter and would be supportive.

"You weren't going behind my back," Maddie said, looking over at Josie.

"That's what I've been trying to tell you," Josie said. "Every conversation I've had with Kayla about you has been to tell her what a great mom she has and that she needs to go to you."

Tears ran down Maddie's face. "My jealousy of you has sure put me in a lot of hot water, hasn't it?"

Josie put her arm around Maddie. "Yes. And we've got to stop this. Today, it almost cost you your daughter and has put a serious dent in your relationship with both Kayla and Brady."

Maddie leaned into her, more tears rolling down her face. "Why don't you hate me more? I just admitted that the whole reason you and Brady aren't together is because I lied about the night I spent with him."

Though Josie hadn't had time to analyze that particular bombshell, she could feel God working in her heart, and as she spoke, she knew it was God's truth coming out.

"None of us can ever fully understand how the Lord works, but if you hadn't lied about Brady being Kayla's father, what kind of upbringing would Kayla have had? I'm assuming her biological father has been nowhere in the picture."

Maddie sniffed. "He was a man I met at a party, and we went too far. He was only here visiting, and I didn't even know his last name, and all I knew was his nickname. By the time I found out I was pregnant, he was gone, and I had no way of contacting him or figuring out who he was."

Remembering what Maddie had told her about not knowing her own father, Josie said, "So had you not lied, Kayla would have grown up like you, without a father. I don't condone the lie, and yes, it caused a lot of harm, but I think Kayla's life was made better for it, don't you?"

Maddie sniffled again as she nodded. "Brady is the best father. I couldn't have chosen a better father for Kayla than him. He sacrificed a lot for her, and his love for her was so apparent from the day he made that commitment to be her father. I wanted that for my little girl, and the longer I carried on that lie, the harder it's been to tell the truth."

Though part of her still wanted to throttle Maddie for being so selfish, she thought about how Brady had always told her the sacrifices he'd made for Kayla were worth it because he loved his daughter. Maddie had hurt them, but Kayla was better off for it.

"I forgive you, Maddie," Josie said. "You still have to deal with Brady and Kayla, but I want you to know that I harbor no grudges against you. Not only has Kayla had a better life because of your lie, but I was also forced into making decisions for my own that brought me a better life."

Once again, Josie felt God's presence and could see God's hands on her life as she continued. "I found the courage to defy my father and run off to college because I couldn't handle seeing you and Brady together. Brady and I had made many plans, and we both hoped to go to college, but I don't know if we would have. Having gone to college and spent time working for the rec center, I learned how to work with youth and help them through their problems because I hadn't had that. And now, all of those things are coming together so that, number one, I appreciate the stables more, and number two, I have the tools necessary to save them. All of that is because of your lie."

Tears were streaming down Maddie's face. "But can Brady forgive me? Can Kayla?"

"I can't speak for them, but I do know if God can give me the strength to forgive my father and forgive you and, most of all, forgive myself, then I believe it's possible for you, too."

Maddie leaned into her, sobbing again. "How can God, or anyone else, love me?"

It was strange to be having this conversation with a woman who had been her enemy for so long. Even though Josie had spent so much time away from God, she knew the answer.

"Because God loves us all. Even when we turn our backs on Him, even when we do wrong. Jesus forgave Judas and all the others who betrayed Him, and His last moments on the cross were about forgiveness, so, of course, He loves you."

Maddie looked up at her. "All the lies you've told me, I know some of the things you've given me proof of, but I have to know. What is the truth?"

Taking a deep breath, Josie asked for God's wisdom once again. This whole conversation, she'd been relying on Him, and He hadn't steered her wrong yet.

"I have never lied to you," Josie said. "I did not start or spread the rumors that you were pregnant. The first time I heard them was when I was in the restroom and others were talking about it, and you came bursting in yelling at us all. I did not purposely have you pitch the tent on that anthill. Your friend Jessica told me to, but I wanted a spot closer to the fire, so I told her if it was so great, then you guys should put your tents there."

Maddie sniffled and looked up at her. "I picked a really bad person to be best friends with, didn't I?"

"Maybe. I'm sure you have some good memories of her. Hanging on to the bad memories of the stables created a bitterness inside me that wasn't healthy. Remember the good things about her, and don't let the negative get you down."

Josie could see the same understanding in Maddie's eyes that she'd seen that day at church when she'd thought they'd fixed things between them.

"Brady and I were telling the truth about our relationship. The kiss you saw was the first time we acknowledged our feelings for each other. As part of that conversation, we both agreed to take it slow and that wherever our relationship went, Kayla was our top priority."

"I've accused you of a lot, haven't I?"

Josie took a deep breath. "Yes, but the question is, how can we put all of this behind us once and for all?"

"I'm going to try," Maddie said. She gestured at Josie's phone. "Thanks for sharing Kayla's email with me. I feel bad that I missed it, but now I know why she's been so grouchy with me. She thought I was ignoring her when I just hadn't checked my email."

Maddie sighed, then looked over at Josie. "How am I supposed to make things right with Kayla? I messed up big-time. I know that. But I'm not sure where to go from here."

After today's events, Josie could understand why Maddie was feeling so out of sorts. The emotionally charged confrontations, and even this moment of healing, had taken a lot out of all of them.

"Can I make some suggestions?"

She asked because she wasn't sure if things had been repaired enough between them for her to be in a position to give advice, but hopefully, she could make a difference in this situation.

Maddie wiped her nose on her sleeve and said, "Sure. What do I have to lose at this point?"

Josie put her arm around the other woman and gave her a slight side hug. "First and foremost, pray. Talk to God. I firmly believe that the biggest difference made in my situation with the stables was when I told God that even though what we wanted was for the stables to be saved, we were prepared to accept His will, whatever it was. Yes, I want the stables to be saved, but it's made me seek God on a deeper level. That's what you need."

Maddie nodded. "You're right. The truth is, I haven't been relying on God much lately. When I saw you meeting with that developer, and I thought it was proof that the reconciliation between us and everything you've been saying and doing was fake, I didn't take it to God. I relied on myself and my investigation to prove once and for all that you weren't who you said you were."

The sincerity in Maddie's voice gave Josie hope. Maddie continued, "I was fueled by the pain of the past and not God's word. I didn't even try to seek a biblical reconciliation. I just charged ahead without thinking. I'm sorry."

Josie squeezed Maddie. "I accept your apology. The important thing is that we're going to try again and do better at communicating."

She took a deep breath, turning her attention back to Maddie. "Which leads me to my next piece of advice. You should seek out a counselor, both for yourself and to help bring restoration to your family. There is still real fallout that you need to deal with. A good therapist will help you through that. Together, with the help of God, I know you'll come through this better than ever."

Before Maddie could answer, Josie heard the sound of an ATV approaching.

"That must be our rescue crew," Josie said.

"Thank you for staying with me until they came. You could have left me, especially since I told you to. You have every right to hate me, and you chose to love me instead."

Josie smiled at the other woman as she got to her feet to flag down the ATVs. "It's what Jesus did. But also, I've had people like Abigail and other women in the church who have shown me that kind of love. Hating each other hasn't solved anything or made anything better, so love has to be the answer."

One of the rescue workers pulled up next to them and got off the ATV. "Let's make sure you're not injured, Maddie, and we'll get you back to the stables. Your horse has already found his way back and was eager for his grain."

Perchibald whinnied in the distance, reminding Josie she still had other responsibilities.

"I need to get him put away. I'll see you

soon," Josie said. After conferring with the rescue workers, Josie got on the horse and headed home. She might not be getting her happy ending with Brady, but today felt like a victory regardless. Kayla was safe, and while the truth was painful, it had been finally brought to light, and they could all move toward healing.

Chapter Twelve

In the week that followed Kayla running off, Brady had barely seen Josie. Probably for the best, considering he wasn't sure how he could keep his distance from her on a romantic level, not when what he needed most was for her to take him in her arms and tell him that everything was going to be okay.

Kayla had been staying at his house, not speaking to Maddie. At least until today, when they finally got in to see the family therapist Pastor Cline had recommended. He'd left the session feeling hopeful because Maddie had accepted fault for her actions and given a sincere apology to their daughter. Though Kayla was still angry, she had agreed to give her mother the chance to make it up to her.

How, he didn't know, since Maddie had no idea who Kayla's biological father was. Though Brady had told Kayla he would always be her dad, his daughter wanted answers that no one could give her. But at least they were moving forward.

Now he was on his way to the volunteer committee meeting, where Maddie had agreed to apologize to the committee for drawing conclusions and making a public confrontation without all the information. Josie was finally going to share about the opportunity for the stables to bid on having the rec-center programs use their facilities for the summer.

So all was moving forward in a good way, except for the ache in Brady's heart.

The meeting convened as usual, and Brady was surprised to see Maddie sitting next to Josie. The women appeared friendly toward each other, and it warmed his heart. Maddie had said in the counseling session that she and Josie had worked through their issues, but Brady had thought that had happened before, so hopefully, this time, it worked.

"I know we usually begin with an update from the committee members, but in the spirit of healing and reconciliation, Maddie has asked to address the committee."

Josie squeezed Maddie before Maddie stood, and it broke his heart in a small way, knowing that he could not have Josie's love for himself. They'd done the right thing, though, ending their relationship so Brady could focus on Kayla and Maddie.

"Last week, I made some accusations against Josie," Maddie said. "I thought I had done my research, but it turns out I was wrong. Josie didn't sign any contracts to sell the stables. Her father did. But he died before it could be executed, and the buyer, Josie's uncle, having seen Josie's passion for revitalizing the stables, has agreed to back out of the deal and is sponsoring our show instead."

Her gaze rested on Brady for a moment, then went to Josie, where it remained. "I sincerely apologize for the drama I caused needlessly. But I wanted to publicly give my commitment to this project and to my unwavering belief in Josie and her desire to save the stables."

As Maddie turned to leave the podium, the people in the stands applauded. He could see the tears in Maddie's eyes, and Josie went to her and hugged her before they sat. When Brady retook the podium, he could see the impact Maddie's words had made on the audience. There seemed to be a renewed energy and excitement about the project, and he knew they would be able to move forward together.

Brady continued through the agenda, giving Josie the floor when it was time to explain the summer program. Though it had been only a week since she'd first come up with the idea, she'd done her homework and had a very clear plan to present. She'd be sharing the same presentation with the rec-center people later this week, and he had to say, if they weren't impressed, nothing could impress them. When the meeting ended, Brady was convinced that finally, everything was going to work out okay.

He spoke briefly with the various members at the end, noting that both Maddie and Josie had hung back to talk with others as well. Seeing how they all engaged in what seemed to be a positive manner was another sign for Brady that they were headed in the right direction.

When everyone finally cleared the arena, Brady headed to his office, where Maddie was waiting.

"I know that we already did a lot of talking in counseling," she said. "But I needed to let you know how sorry I truly am for everything. I hate that I am the reason you and Josie aren't together. I can't make up for the years I stole from you two, but if you let me, I want to help you have a future with her."

His throat caught at the earnestness in her voice. No, it didn't make up for the years he and Josie weren't together, but as he'd been mulling over with Pastor Cline and praying about it, had Maddie not lied, Brady would not have had all this wonderful time as a father. Kayla was the biggest blessing he'd ever had in his life, and no matter how hard he tried to think about doing it differently, he couldn't. Biology didn't change the fact that she was his daughter.

"Thank you," Brady said. "I know I told you in the counseling session that I was working on forgiving you, but the Bible doesn't tell us to work on forgiveness. It says to do it, so I do. I forgive you."

He wasn't expecting the way he felt lighter having said those words to Maddie, but he did. He hoped he could live them. He'd thought the situation hopeless, but with Maddie's support, they could find a way to work things out.

"Thank you," Maddie said. "Because of

my talk with Josie, I've been seeking the Lord more deeply. Though I've been going to church for a long time, I haven't followed Him the way I ought to have."

She hesitated for a moment, looking like the scared young girl he'd known all those years ago. "We tried to do the romantic thing based on my lie, and that failed miserably. Since then, we've done our best to co-parent Kayla, but we've never actually been friends. I know it's a big ask, but do you think we could try that?"

Maddie's words hit him hard, like a thousand-pound horse coming at him full force. She was right. They had always been polite and cordial and worked together as a team for Kayla's sake, but they hadn't ever tried to work on their relationship.

"I'm sorry," she said. "That was a dumb idea. After everything I've done to you, I shouldn't have asked."

Brady took a step toward her. "No. That was the perfect thing to ask and the one thing we've never tried. Maddie Antere, would you please be my friend?"

He held out his arms to Maddie and hugged her tight to him. In all these years, they had never done this. Even when they thought they would try to get married for Kayla's sake, affection between them had been minimal and felt weird. But to finally build a relationship based on truth and God's love, this felt right.

As he broke off the hug, Josie stepped into the office.

"I'm sorry, I didn't mean to interrupt," she said.

Maddie turned toward her. "You didn't. You came at a great time. You said you wouldn't be in a relationship with Brady because you didn't want to interfere with our family. But Brady and I just made a decision that we'd never made before, and we're going to be friends. And friends look out for each other."

Maddie looked at Josie, then over at Brady. "You're both my friends, and as I just told Brady, I made some dumb mistakes in keeping the two of you apart."

The vulnerability on her face was unlike anything he'd ever seen from her before. He glanced over at Josie, who had tears in her eyes. For Josie, facing her childhood bully and hearing this kind of talk had to be an incredible change for her.

"I am so sorry for everything I did against the two of you," Maddie said. "Josie, you said that in your relationship with Brady, you were going to put his daughter first. I believe you. And as Kayla's mother, I know that what her dad needs most is a woman who will stand by his side and fight for him and what's right the way you have. I promise both of you that our family is me, Brady, Kayla and Josie from this moment on. Can we all work together?"

If Brady hadn't already had a lump in his throat, seeing the tears in Josie's eyes would have put one there.

"What happens if we have a conflict?" Josie asked. "We'd found a place of forgiveness once before, and then it all blew up. What's to say it's not going to happen again?"

The courage and fear in Josie's voice made Brady want to take her in his arms and tell her that they'd figure it out together, but this was Maddie's show, and he knew that this was something Maddie had to do.

"Then we'll work it out," Maddie said. "When I think back on those hours of worry at not finding Kayla, I knew that it was my stupid pride that had caused all that trouble. That's something I'm working on because I can't hurt my daughter ever again. She means too much to me."

Kayla came into the room. "Do you mean that?"

"Yes, I do," Maddie said. "I have made so many mistakes. I am so sorry. I thought I was doing it all for you, but I was very selfish in my actions, and I'm trying to make it right, starting with trying to help your dad and Josie get back together."

Brady looked over at Josie to see her reaction and saw that she had allowed a few tears to escape. Did she have any idea how beautiful she was?

"I didn't mean it when I said that I wished Josie was my mom instead of you," Kayla said. "Other than the fact that you lied to me about my dad, you're a pretty great mom. But I hope Josie and my dad get together because Josie would be a pretty awesome stepmom."

The old Maddie would have flipped out at such a statement. Since he'd been the victim of Maddie's tirades when he dated anyone else, Brady would know.

But this Maddie held her arms out to Kayla and said, "I couldn't think of anything better. Why don't we leave these two alone to talk, and you and I can go get ice cream or pedicures or something."

The smile Kayla gave her mother told

Brady that they were well on their way to figuring things out as a family. The question was, was this enough to convince Josie to give him another chance?

When they left, Brady locked the door so they wouldn't be interrupted again.

"I know that's a lot to take in," he said. "But I believe Maddie, and I believe in us. There has to be a reason that God keeps bringing us back together, so this time, I want to make the most of it."

Josie didn't say anything at first, but then she nodded. "I think you're right. Part of me is terrified that we'll have a setback with Maddie or Kayla, but the other part of me is reminded that God has been faithful, and no matter what, He'll be there supporting us."

Brady breached the distance between them and held her tight in his arms. "Unlike how we prayed for the stables, I'm not praying for any other options. You are my only option, and I'm going to do whatever it takes to make our relationship work."

Instead of answering with words, Josie reached her arms up to his neck and pulled him close to her, kissing him. Her touch was beautiful and glorious, and though the kisses they'd shared as teenagers had all been wonderful, this spoke of something deeper and more real. This kiss was the promise of forever after having been through life trials and understanding that forever would take a lot of hard work, commitment and trust in God.

But when they broke off the kiss and he looked at the love shining in her eyes, he had absolute faith that they would make their relationship and their family work.

Epilogue

As Josie sat in the announcer's box the day of the show, every nerve in her body tingled with excitement.

Yesterday, she had been told that the rec center had accepted the stables' bid to be their summer horseback-riding contractor. It would provide the stables with a steady income that more than covered their operating expenses, and thanks to the suggestions and vision of her team, Josie would be able to work from the stables and only have to go into the office a couple of times a month. Josie's presentation had been such a hit that the rec center wanted to explore the idea of going back to the many horse programs they used to offer but couldn't because they didn't have anyone who could provide the horseback-riding services.

She scanned the audience to see members of the board of directors of the rec center sitting there. After touring the facility, they'd wanted to see the show so they could see the range of what the stables could do.

The sound of someone entering the announcer's booth made her turn. Brady was supposed to be here, but he texted saying that there was a problem in the barn and he was running late. Instead of Brady's smiling face, she saw Hal. In his hands, she spied a familiar binder she thought had been lost.

"Is that my father's show binder?"

Hal grinned. "Yep. He gave it to me for safekeeping a while back."

"Why didn't you say anything? I could have used that to plan the show."

Handing her the binder, Hal said, "I know. But I wanted you to make this show yours. Following your father's binder would have spoiled that. But I think it's time you have it."

Growing up, her father's binder had been one of those things she'd never been allowed to touch because it was so special to him. She had always thought that he never let her see it because he was afraid that it would give away show secrets or special information about the lineup that he didn't want her to have as an advantage over the other girls.

But when she opened the binder, its contents surprised her. The first section was exactly what she thought it would be. A list of the show lineups and acts, and a script for announcing the show. But when she flipped to the second tab, it was like a scrapbook of sorts, where he'd stuck pictures with comments. Not the critical words she'd been used to hearing growing up, but things like "her best performance yet."

Her eyes filled with tears as she realized that in this binder, her father was saying all the things she'd longed to hear from him.

Josie looked over at Hal. "Why couldn't he have told me all this while he was alive?"

Hal shrugged. "Your grandfather taught him that praise made a person weak. Your father thought he was making you stronger and better by pointing out your flaws and ways of improving. I used to get on him about that, but you know your father, always having to do things his way."

As Josie flipped through the pages, memories flooded back to her. How she wished things had been different between them. All this time, she thought that her father didn't love her, but the pages of this book, where he'd taken notes about her and her performances, told a very different story. Her father loved her.

She closed the book and went over to Hal, giving him a big hug. "Thank you for giving this to me. I wish I'd known about it a long time ago, but I'm glad to have it now."

Hal hugged her back, then said, "I thought about giving it to you the day of the will reading, but you were so angry, I don't think you would have appreciated it the way you do now. Your father had a lot of flaws, but I hope now you'll see the good side of him, too."

Josie nodded and hugged Hal again, even though he was your typical old-school cowboy who didn't like to show affection. After the hug, he brushed her off, and said, "That's enough of that. I won't have anyone thinking I'm getting soft. I'm gonna go find my seat so I can enjoy the show."

Brady finally entered as he was leaving. "What was that about? Hal was rubbing his eyes, mentioning something about keeping the dust down."

Josie smiled at the man she loved. "Did you know he had my dad's show binder?"

She opened it to the pictures of her, and Brady looked surprised. "Nope. Another one of his secrets, I guess."

"I guess," Josie said. "It's just a shame that he thought that showing me too much love and affection would make me weak. Had I known how much he loved me, it would have made me stronger. But how sad that's all he knew, so I guess this has to be enough."

Brady put his arms around her. "When it comes to our family, we're going to do better. We've both learned how destructive secrets can be and the incredible power of God's love in transforming lives. From this moment on, that's what our family will be known for."

Josie felt his warmth as she hugged him tightly, thanking God for a man who was willing to love even when it was hard.

She pulled away, then smiled up at him. "It's funny how we've barely been back together for a month, and you're already talking about our family."

"As I told you when we decided to have this relationship, there are no other options for me. I intended to do this later, after the show, and after I announced that we had exceeded our fundraising goal for the show, but I can't wait any longer."

He pulled a box out of his pocket, and Josie knew exactly what it was.

"Brady…"

He got down on one knee and held the box out to her. "A little over fifteen years ago, we promised each other that when you graduated high school, we were going to get married and make a life for ourselves away from this place. While I appreciate the sentiment of those two lovesick kids, my plans have changed. I want to build a life with you, right here, at these stables. I'm hoping you'll join me."

"Yes," she said. "We aren't those kids anymore. Though I believe we knew back then what love was, we now understand the richness and the depths of all the things love can be. And I don't want to be anywhere else."

When she opened the ring box, it wasn't the old familiar ring they'd talked about Brady putting on her finger someday.

"Back then, that cheap diamond was all I could afford. It wasn't much, but it was enough. So I took that diamond ring to the jewelers, and I had it reset with two other diamonds. Our old diamond represents our past, the center diamond represents our present and the other diamond is our future."

When he slipped the ring on her finger,

Josie couldn't imagine anything more perfect. Though the journey had been difficult, as she kissed her fiancé, she believed it was completely worth it.

A knock sounded at the door. "Dad!"

Brady chuckled as he gave Josie another quick kiss, then opened the door.

"Yes, Miss Impatient?"

Kayla entered the room, and her eyes immediately alighted on Josie's hand. "That wasn't the plan," she said. "And you call me impatient."

Maddie entered the room, chuckling. "But we knew this is how it was going to end. Now congratulate them so we can get back downstairs and get you into your costume."

Once Maddie had looked at Kayla's presentation, she'd agreed that her daughter had a knack for costume design. The trick riders all wore costumes designed by Kayla, and Maddie was looking into classes for Kayla to continue her passion.

Kayla hugged Brady, then turned to Josie and hugged her. "I'm glad you're part of my family," she said.

"Okay, now go," Maddie said.

"How did you know I was proposing?" Brady asked. "You guys were in on the plan for me to do it after the show, but how did you know I was doing it now?"

Maddie gestured out the window to the stands. "We all saw you getting down on one knee. I have not run this fast to get here since I was a teenager."

"You didn't have to be part of this," Brady said.

"Yes, I did," Maddie said. "I had to make sure that Josie knew she had our absolute blessing in becoming part of this family."

When Josie hugged Maddie, she felt so much warmth from her new friend...no, her family member. "Thank you," Josie said. "That means a lot. Now, as you so eloquently told your daughter, you're needed to supervise costumes. And I have a show to run, so let's get to it."

Maddie left, and the announcer box filled with the people needed to put on the show. Though Josie had done everything she needed to run the program, when it finished, she couldn't have told anyone a single thing that happened during it, other than everything was a perfect success.

She could count on something going wrong, usually something minor, but it was always enough to get her heart rate up. If any of that happened with this show, Josie couldn't have said. With her father's binder staying in front of her, the man she loved by her side and her future stepdaughter flawlessly performing in the arena, Josie finally had the life she'd always wanted. The details might differ from what she had originally planned, but this was so much better.

* * * * *

Dear Reader,

A funny thing always happens to me when I write a book. It seems like one of the messages my character struggles with is something that God points out to me as something I also need to deal with in my own life. Forgiveness is hard, especially as we carry old wounds from the past. But as I've learned, and as Josie and Maddie learned, holding on to them doesn't do us any good. However, letting go of those things brings us unimaginable freedom, and the process of struggling with them helps us grow closer to God.

I hope that whatever challenge you struggle with, you know you're not alone. God is with you, even in the darkest moments when you think you can't see Him. But more than that, I hope you know that there are other people, like me, who often struggle with the same things. You are not alone. Take heart and know that you are deeply loved.

Feel free to reach out to me at any time through my website at danicafavorite.com.

From my heart to yours,
Danica Favorite

Get 4 FREE REWARDS!

We'll send you 2 FREE Books plus 2 FREE Mystery Gifts.

FREE
Value Over
$20

Both the **Love Inspired®** and **Love Inspired® Suspense** series feature compelling novels filled with inspirational romance, faith, forgiveness, and hope.

YES! Please send me 2 FREE novels from the Love Inspired or Love Inspired Suspense series and my 2 FREE gifts (gifts are worth about $10 retail). After receiving them, if I don't wish to receive any more books, I can return the shipping statement marked "cancel." If I don't cancel, I will receive 6 brand-new Love Inspired Larger-Print books or Love Inspired Suspense Larger-Print books every month and be billed just $6.24 each in the U.S. or $6.49 each in Canada. That is a savings of at least 17% off the cover price. It's quite a bargain! Shipping and handling is just 50¢ per book in the U.S. and $1.25 per book in Canada.* I understand that accepting the 2 free books and gifts places me under no obligation to buy anything. I can always return a shipment and cancel at any time by calling the number below. The free books and gifts are mine to keep no matter what I decide.

Choose one: ☐ **Love Inspired**
　　　　　　　　Larger-Print
　　　　　　　　(122/322 IDN GRDF)

☐ **Love Inspired Suspense**
　　Larger-Print
　　(107/307 IDN GRDF)

Name (please print)

Address   Apt. #

City   State/Province   Zip/Postal Code

Email: Please check this box ☐ if you would like to receive newsletters and promotional emails from Harlequin Enterprises ULC and its affiliates. You can unsubscribe anytime.

Mail to the **Harlequin Reader Service:**
IN U.S.A.: P.O. Box 1341, Buffalo, NY 14240-8531
IN CANADA: P.O. Box 603, Fort Erie, Ontario L2A 5X3

Want to try 2 free books from another series! Call 1-800-873-8635 or visit www.ReaderService.com.

---

*Terms and prices subject to change without notice. Prices do not include sales taxes, which will be charged (if applicable) based on your state or country of residence. Canadian residents will be charged applicable taxes. Offer not valid in Quebec. This offer is limited to one order per household. Books received may not be as shown. Not valid for current subscribers to the Love Inspired or Love Inspired Suspense series. All orders subject to approval. Credit or debit balances in a customer's account(s) may be offset by any other outstanding balance owed by or to the customer. Please allow 4 to 6 weeks for delivery. Offer available while quantities last.

Your Privacy—Your information is being collected by Harlequin Enterprises ULC, operating as Harlequin Reader Service. For a complete summary of the information we collect, how we use this information and to whom it is disclosed, please visit our privacy notice located at corporate.harlequin.com/privacy-notice. From time to time we may also exchange your personal information with reputable third parties. If you wish to opt out of this sharing of your personal information, please visit readerservice.com/consumerschoice or call 1-800-873-8635. **Notice to California Residents**—Under California law, you have specific rights to control and access your data. For more information on these rights and how to exercise them, visit corporate.harlequin.com/california-privacy.

LIRLIS22R2

COUNTRY LEGACY COLLECTION

19 FREE BOOKS IN ALL!

Cowboys, adventure and romance await you in this new collection! Enjoy superb reading all year long with books by bestselling authors like Diana Palmer, Sasha Summers and Marie Ferrarella!

YES! Please send me the **Country Legacy Collection!** This collection begins with 3 FREE books and 2 FREE gifts in the first shipment. Along with my 3 free books, I'll also get 3 more books from the **Country Legacy Collection**, which I may either return and owe nothing or keep for the low price of $24.60 U.S./$28.12 CDN each plus $2.99 U.S./$7.49 CDN for shipping and handling per shipment*. If I decide to continue, about once a month for 8 months, I will get 6 or 7 more books but will only pay for 4. That means 2 or 3 books in every shipment will be FREE! If I decide to keep the entire collection, I'll have paid for only 32 books because 19 are FREE! I understand that accepting the 3 free books and gifts places me under no obligation to buy anything. I can always return a shipment and cancel at any time. My free books and gifts are mine to keep no matter what I decide.

☐ 275 HCK 1939   ☐ 475 HCK 1939

Name (please print)

Address   Apt. #

City   State/Province   Zip/Postal Code

Mail to the Harlequin Reader Service:
IN U.S.A.: P.O. Box 1341, Buffalo, NY 14240-8571
IN CANADA: P.O. Box 603, Fort Erie, Ontario L2A 5X3